Gross Margin

Gross Margin

Laurent Quintreau

Translated
from
the French
by
Polly McLean

HARVILL SECKER
LONDON

Published by Harvill Secker 2008

2 4 6 8 10 9 7 5 3 1

First published with the title *Marge brute* in 2006
by Éditions Denoël, Paris

First published in Great Britain in 2008 by
HARVILL SECKER
Random House, 20 Vauxhall Bridge Road,
London SW1V 2SA

www.rbooks.co.uk

Addresses for companies within
The Penguin Random House Group can be found at:
global.penguinrandomhouse.com

The Random House Group Limited Reg. No. 954009

A CIP catalogue record for this book is available from the British Library

ISBN 9781787301542

This book is supported by the French Ministry of Foreign Affairs, as part of the
Burgess programme run by the Cultural Department of the French Embassy in London.
www.frenchbooknews.com

Liberté · Égalité · Fraternité
RÉPUBLIQUE FRANÇAISE

Ouvrage publié avec le soutien du Centre national du livre – ministère français chargé de la
culture.
This book is published with support from the French Ministry of Culture – Centre National
du Livre.

MIX
Paper | Supporting
responsible forestry
FSC® C018179

Printed and bound in Great Britain by Clays Ltd, Elcograf S.p.A.

The quotation reproduced opposite is from Dorothy Sayers' translation
of *The Divine Comedy* published by Penguin Classics in 1950

Midway this way of life we're bound upon
I woke to find myself in a dark wood,
Where the right road was wholly lost and gone.

DANTE ALIGHIERI, *The Divine Comedy*

To V.
For J.

Contents

11am: eleven executives
around a boardroom table.

Hell

1st circle (limbo): Meyer

. . . right, Rorty has arrived, we're all here, the meeting can start, I'm not scared, no longer scared, my files are all up to date and my accounts in the black, my heart has stopped hammering, those beta blockers really work, OK, Rorty has sat down, the meeting can start, Rorty is wearing a white shirt and a smart navy suit with thin charcoal pinstripes, his greying brown hair swept backwards like some cheesy TV lawyer, his tie is terracotta with a tiny yellow motif, what is it, hard to see, beetles, no, tennis balls, yes, tennis balls, Rorty modulates his voice, bids everyone welcome, thanks us all for putting aside our daily tasks to attend this strategy committee, still a bit of heartburn, shouldn't drink so much coffee, try to keep it to three a day, two in the morning and one after lunch, Rorty is repeating how important it is that the managers here today feel invested in the running of the company, a company which has had a great year, with more than fifteen per cent operating margin last quarter, but which must build on this growth, now more than ever, now is not the time to lower our guard, we must work harder, smarter – I'm afraid, says clever Rorty wryly, that we are all condemned to excellence, several people smile, Pujol sniggers, Brémont fidgets on her chair, Castaglione looks knowing, sly, with her beady little eyes and pointy, fox-like nose, Tissier nods half-heartedly, de Vals cracks a big shifty grin, Stoeffer frowns, Françoise Clément-Dourville sighs, Roussel stares at the table, Alighieri has a strange, blissful smile on his face, not bad that boy, always reminds me of David, same kind of face, same way of being, moving and speaking, same intensity when he looks at you, David, at least he knew how to love, too much perhaps, so jealous, so possessive, so ardent, it ended up stifling me, if only I'd been brave enough to confront him, rather than just leaving in the night like a thief, we'd still be together, I wouldn't have met Denis, wouldn't be working here, we'd still be living in New York, I'd have had some other little girl instead of Chloë, or perhaps a boy, I'd be living in a pretty house in Greenwich village, surrounded by green space, trees, Rorty keeps repeating how he intends to haul the company up into the top levels of competitiveness and expertise, make us the sector leaders, yes, the leaders in corporate communications, but for this we'll have to keep increasing our market share, winning new clients, being the most aggressive, the keenest, it's a matter of life or death for the company as for the people in it, we're all in the same boat, our results are encouraging but the market remains hostile, the future uncertain to say the least, and the over-heads heavy, very heavy, not to mention the wage bill, alas, we are all in the same boat but if the boat is too low in the water everyone will drown, restructuring a company means picking out the best, nothing but the best, I hope Chloë likes her new nanny, with the last one she used to scream that she didn't want to stay with the horrid lady, she used to cling to me, it was awful, and yet the woman didn't seem like a torturer, but then who knows what goes on in children's minds, Rorty is reminding us that he's been running the company for not much more than a year, congratulating himself on the degree of change already achieved, but there is a great deal still to do, yes, there is good, even excellent potential, borne out by the figures it seems, a fifteen per cent operating margin, almost ten million of gross margin in the last financial year, there is talent, there is determination, but our share price is being hobbled by massive energy wastage and outrageous inefficiencies, the group has planned a substantial reduction in the workforce and wage bill of all its subsidiaries by 2008, enabling it to pay off its debt and continue a policy of external growth, this has all been decided by the board, it's what the shareholders want, one thing is for sure, this group takes its shareholders seriously, Rorty was parachuted in by New York to transform the company into a dividend drip-feed under the close eye of the holding company, Big Money is watching you, Rorty is on fire, it's vital to boost the process, reinvigorate the flow, we have won new clients, new prospects have, as recently as this morning – he and de Vals exchange a knowing look – responded favourably to our proposals but there's a lot more to do to optimise the volume of new business, there's still, that is to say, everything to play for to become – let's not beat around the bush, although the word is overused and may seem hackneyed – the best, my back hurts, sciatica perhaps, let's hope not, quick, ask Alex for her osteopath's number, he's excellent apparently, Stoeffer's having a phlegmy coughing fit building up to a revolting noise from deep within, ugh, he disgusts me, I feel sick, Rorty stares at him with fake compassion, Rorty is an attractive man, trim for forty, Paris-New York-Courchevel-Neuilly, Rorty watches what he eats, Stoeffer smokes more than forty fags a day and eats for four, all the steak, chips and profiteroles he happens to fancy, not to mention the whisky stashed in his office cupboard, Stoeffer will die twenty years younger than Rorty, could be anything, cancer, heart attack, Alighieri is looking at Rorty with affection, yes, affection, astonishing but true, he seems to be gazing at Stoeffer with great kindness too, Alighieri, to think that I dreamt about him last night, wearing a stovepipe hat and with a small white dog on a lead, it was barking at a cloud, I also remember a car, a black BMW with tinted windows, then everything speeded up, I can't remember what happened, I think Alighieri was levitating next to the car, yes, I can see him now, radiant and still, like one of those illumi-nated saints you see in Romanesque churches, dream or no dream this Alighieri is an enigma, he's even more bizarre than usual today, must spend his evenings smoking pot, Rorty is more and more lit up by the power of his own speech, his steely blue eyes boring into those of everyone present,

Rorty's intensity is penetrating their flesh, their desires, their fears, Rorty learnt the basic rules of management while studying at Harvard, you can't make an omelette without breaking some eggs, on this adventure we'll be able to retain only the best, that's the law of the free market, as you know, I know that you know, you know that I know that you know but there are some basics one never tires of repeating, he concludes, before moving on to the first item on the day's agenda, staff cutbacks in the legal department, his eyes are still just as cold, the idea of paring back the wage bill seems to neither bother nor entertain him, deep down he terrifies me, I don't dare stand up to him because I sense extreme violence behind his polished Wasp façade, the man is a pitiless predator, there's something implacable about him that I find very frightening, and also I don't want to be fired, how could we pay our mortgage on one salary, or the car or all our other bills, no, impossible, Stoeffer's moustache is shaking with anger, he reminds me of someone, who is it, he has plonked himself right opposite Rorty, the two men are staring at each other again, oh yes, that's it, Honoré de Balzac, Stoeffer reminds me of Honoré de Balzac towards the end of his life, he has the same kind of face, epicurean and at the same time explosive, and the moustache, of course, the moustache, hey, rereading *The Human Comedy* would take my mind off things, or Flaubert, why not Flaubert, never managed to finish *Madame Bovary*, I just need to find time, last thing at night perhaps, Rorty is picking on Françoise, where have you got to since our last meeting my dear Françoise, what's happened with the two forthcoming retirements, Françoise straightens up nervously on her chair, the two women have made enquiries about their rights, they no longer want to leave, the payments offered by the company are not adequate, they want proper financial compensation, they've nothing to lose, they are prepared to resort to a lawyer, at the word lawyer Rorty frowns and then smoothes out his face, crosses and uncrosses his legs, readjusts his shirt and folds his arms, all in the blink of an eye, his tone becomes ironic, biting, unless I am very much mistaken, it's not the employees who decide whether or not they remain in the company and to what payment they may aspire when they leave, Françoise looks so exhausted, he's putting her under such pressure, and her husband is dying, I don't want to be like that in twenty years, actually what will I be doing, where will I be in twenty years, just thinking about it makes me feel depressed, Rorty is snorting like a horse, fine, fine, his eyes shine a little brighter, if these employees want to play hardball, we will too – I want you to overload them with work, force them to make mistakes, and when they do something serious they'll go straight to the labour relations authorities, which rarely recommend more than a year and a half's salary, even after thirty years' service, Françoise explains that it is now harder to lay off staff aged fifty and over because of the Delalande contribution – any company that dismisses someone over fifty has to pay it, that's the law, Rorty is seething, fine, fine, long live the right to work, in that case do me a favour and fire the best paid fortysomethings, Françoise has gone white, my god, she looks like a ghost, the rings under her eyes are darkening as I watch, de Vals is staring at her with amused cynicism, Pujol is sniggering stupidly, what an idiot, wavy brown hair, dishwater-grey eyes, regular, rather coarse features, the false attractiveness of the cheap playboy, the podgy, unappetising physique of the pseudo-handsome, Alighieri is still miles away, gazing out of the window at a rainbow none of us can see, imagine if I had a lover, a gentle, charming, attentive man, we'd see each other on certain week nights and some-times at the weekend, he'd be a filmmaker, a theatre director or a writer, living in a split-level apartment on place Saint-Sulpice, we'd meet up on boulevard Saint-Germain to set the world to rights over a drink, walk the streets for hours, pop into an art-house movie in the Latin quarter and finish the evening at his place, his split level apartment, listening to the night and getting to know each other, as naked and carefree as two teenagers discovering love for the first time, come on, just two overpaid fortysomethings, coaxes Rorty, we can take on interns instead, they produce good work if they're properly managed, a third of the minimum wage and already operational, on that note I'd better speak to Sylvie Dumas, the client order forms were littered with mistakes again, the fact that she's going through a divorce is no excuse, I'll have a quiet word, remind her that she is obliged to produce at least some work in exchange for her remuneration, it's in her contract, how much is she paid again, two thousand euros I think, two thousand euros to arrive at ten and leave at six having taken an hour for lunch, not a bad hourly rate, though if I'm going to tell her off I'd better do it gently, I can see her now, playing the victim again, that whole 'helpless assistant plagued by nasty boss' number, last time she threatened to report me to the workplace inspection people for moral damage, as if her own attitude weren't damaging the company, OK, now I'm annoyed, Rorty is watching me, his hair still just as sleek and his eyes as bright, he reminds me of the plate-glass window of an eighties building on the Californian coast, Françoise sighs and puts a hand to her brow, she's run the department for over ten years and has never yet fired a single person, what an ordeal, a superb lawyer too, such a fine, cultured woman but so fragile, once she's cut the dead wood from her department Rorty will get rid of her too, that's for sure, and then what, no joke finding a new job aged fifty-four, any HR director in any company will tell you with a formal smile that despite your personal and professional qualities you don't fit the position, even at forty you're too old to find a new job, it's all over, Rorty is telling Françoise that she has one month to instigate a dismissals procedure against the least productive staff in her department, she protests, she doesn't understand, they all work at least ten hours a day, the files are always dealt with promptly, she has never paid her colleagues to sit around doing nothing, de Vals is shaking his head, he'd like to share his experience regarding interns, the two newest members of his team are recent graduates of the top business schools of he no longer remembers which provincial town, Reims, Nantes, Poitiers, they get through a colossal amount of work, sometimes staying until midnight and never complaining, a company could easily function on pools of well-managed interns in a horizontal but pyramidal structure, de Vals grins, emitting a strange-sounding snigger reminiscent of a hyena or a jackal, yes, more a jackal, Rorty gives him a knowing, well done my son, you'll go far kind of look, Tissier and Brémont nod distractedly, Castaglione sits up straight with a strange kind of sexy, domineering pout, Stoeffer winces, Alighieri is still away with the fairies, Alighieri, Pujol is staring at me, I don't like it, don't like the guy, sex without grace, heavy, cumbersome, an archetypal sports-club don Juan, the Casanova of the changing rooms, he really bothers me, I need to protect myself against his insidious presence, I'm not sure what he reminds me of but I know I don't like it, that dirty, shifty gaze, unwholesome thoughts, mechanical sex, the empty, burlesque obscenity of sex without love, my heartburn is back, the base of my spine is itching, scratch it gently with my pen, ah, that's better, I hope Denis won't be home too late this evening, he really is tired and grumpy these days, it's been so long since anything happened between us, are couples subject to the same rules as companies, fixed-term and permanent contracts, dismissal for professional inadequacy, the day has barely started and I'm already so depressed . . .

13

2nd circle: Pujol

. . . can't wait to see my little pharmacist tonight, in the meantime Dominique Meyer is quite sexy, a little sad, for sure, but very sexy, definitely more sexy than sad, hey, better calm down, she'll notice in a minute, focus on this bloody meeting, I'm chilled, I'm strong, I'm breathing, I won't stutter if Rorty grills me about the account for the state campaign against accidents in the workplace that we were supposed to win, he thinks it's in the bag, OK, so I got a bit ahead of myself by claiming it was signed, or nearly, mea culpa, that's life, it's done now, I'm not exactly going to give myself a public whipping, let's look to the future, opportunities for development, promising prospects, take advantage of that to mention Marc, just in passing, yes, remind Rorty that my brother-in-law is on the board of the country's biggest health provider, isn't that one of the reasons, perhaps the only reason he took me on, I remember his face lighting up when I mentioned Marc during my recruitment interview, you bet, such a great opportunity for the company, bloody Rorty, still going on about settlements, encouraging us to cut the dead wood from our teams but making it clear that he doesn't want to pay for it, two months max for under four years, six months for the longest serving, he's going a bit far there, we're hardly going to ask an employee who's been with us for ten or twenty years to leave with six months' compensation, that's pretty rough, but then, that's his business, I'll pretend to agree, I'm still in my trial period, another month and I'll be OK, I'll finally be able to relax, or at least freewheel, I'm not sure working for this crazy outfit was such a great idea, but then not much choice, didn't want to find myself being paid a pittance in some two-bit company or worse, on the dole, with my lifestyle I really can't afford to mess up, poverty, what a nightmare, smelly tramps, ugly people in crap housing, leprosy, gangrene, putrid diseased skin, luckily Rorty is on my side, for now at least, as long as I've got him by the bollocks with Marc everything will be fine, right, I'd still better concentrate on this fucking meeting and get ready to respond when it comes to me, I'm chilled, I'm strong, I'm breathing, that Stoeffer looks awful, like an angry old bulldog, yes, a scowling, randy old bulldog, granny's neighbour had one, when we visited he was forever slobbering and clinging to our legs, one day he raped another neighbour's male dog, a Maltese, ripped his whole hind-quarters apart, the poor beast was pouring with blood, Rorty is coming to an agenda point on which, he is quite convinced, we will all be united, or at least delighted, he is of course talking about the company weekend planned for September, exact date and place to be confirmed, regarding the date, we should keep the last weekend of September free, tough luck if we wanted to take our Time Off In Lieu then, regarding the place, he's open to suggestions, what about a quick brain-storm, each of us can put forward our ideas, and then we'll vote and go with the most popular, right, who's ready, come on, ladies first, with a gesture intended to be warm and convivial he invites Brémont to start, that fat sow Brémont, she suggests Tunisia, typical, you can tell just by looking at her how much time she's spent in Djerba trying to get laid, I'd have to be completely pissed, or perhaps in a coma, Castaglione would have us all go to Thailand, to the jungle, far from civilisation, nothing like a change of scene to break with old habits, crack our protective shells and give birth to a new group dynamic, Thailand, I might have guessed, I can just imagine her striding through the tropical rainforest in her safari shorts like some scary man-eating backpacker, she's as unpleasant as she is sexy that girl, I wouldn't mind seeing her naked, there, in the middle of us all, Brémont and Meyer attacking her with cucumbers and dildos, a cat fight, now there's a good idea, Brémont, Meyer and Castaglione naked in the mud, I'd be Castaglione's manager and she'd obey my every glance, my every gesture, stand up, sit down, horizontal, she turns me on but I wouldn't want to be her guy, or only for one night, she must be terrifying in private, speaking of which, shall I go to the next K1 fight at Bercy, why not, I think Thierry's got tickets, Tissier is suggesting Senegal, now there's a surprise, what a loser, poor, poor guy, Senegal, whores on tap in the hotel complex, developing country, brothel for the West, I love African women, but coming after losers like Tissier, no thanks, really, de Vals is showing off as usual, he's found the perfect solution, he fidgets around for several seconds before finally coming out with yurts in Uzbekistan, he's thinking sweat lodges, shamanic ritual, the global village, California where he studied, saying whatever comes into his head and then contradicting himself, I don't like him either, the guy isn't wholesome, brings to mind public urinals, Stoeffer immediately takes the opposite view and suggests Switzerland, according to him perfect for corporate teambuilding, he suggests we climb Mont Cervin, pretty strange idea for someone who smokes more than two packs a day, Rorty looks down at him with derision, he'll fire him one day, no question, unless Stoeffer snuffs it first, Clément-Dourville would rather not travel too far, how about Brittany or Normandy, they seem to her far more realistic than these far-off countries, there are hotel complexes on the coast specially designed for this sort of thing, Roussel wouldn't mind seeing the other side of the world, Australia or New Zealand, that crazy Alighieri responds that Australia would be great but Brittany too, and after all why not Uzbekistan or Thailand, the guy's got no ideas of his own, or else he really doesn't give a shit, Dominique Meyer could see herself in a Mediterranean country like Italy or Greece, strange chick, you never know what she's thinking, always measured, voice never rises, without a doubt the most stirring of this noble assembly with her weary manner, drawling voice and huge knockers, bound to be married but hey, until proven to the contrary that's never stopped me from envisaging a closer collaboration, anyway, why are they all looking at me like that, ah, it's my turn, perhaps I'll say the same thing as Dominique Meyer, no, the Amazon, in any case I'm the improv king, come on, here we go, (. . . . .), I think I did fine, I made them laugh with my suggestion of a *Survivor* remake among the Jivaro Indians, survival lessons during the day, hallucinogenic plants at night, now that's what I call corporate teambuilding, chemical ecstasy and group orgies, who would I start with, Meyer, Castaglione or that fat Brémont, oh, stupid me, I forgot, all the female heads of department and their PAs will be there too, that tall blonde I met at the coffee machine, a bit of a tart, just my type, delicious, can't get enough of them, like that little trainee hairdresser from the 55 club, great in bed but then after, Jesus, I was dying for earplugs, almost fainting with boredom, god that girl was dull, and venal to boot, your job pays pretty well doesn't it, do you like kids, how about a house in the country, I saw her coming a mile off, lucky I wore a condom, I've already made the mistake of getting married, absolutely no desire to end up like that poor Christophe Baltus, how many have I had now, two hundred I think, yes, two hundred and one counting tonight's little pharmacist, two hundred and one and that's just a start, you'll see my lovelies, I'm going to make you all dizzy with pleasure, I'll still be going strong in ten years, twenty years, thirty years, but for that I'd better earn well, no question, cash is my main advantage, black, white, redheads, all ripe for the taking, what about Rorty, hey, I could do it with him, that would be cool, I can just imagine him writhing around, he must be strong, tense, not an easy catch, no, I'm joking, I've never really been attracted to men, I'm an inveterate heterosexual, isn't that right my loves, hey, that message from Jean-Patrick, am I going to the rugby tomorrow night, good question, wish he hadn't asked, all depends on how I'm feeling tomorrow, hard to know, hard to know how tonight will turn out, Rorty is bringing the brainstorm to a close, commenting on our suggestions, he's pretty blunt, Tunisia is a bit trashy for a corporate communications company, Thailand is much too far away, too expensive, hard to organise and would take too long, same goes for Senegal, not to mention the malaria risk, etc etc, Uzbekistan and the Amazon are great ideas in theory but just as unrealistic, Italy or Greece could work, that's worth thinking about, as for Brittany or Normandy, Jesus, Rorty shuts his eyes, runs a gentle hand over his handsome receding executive hairline, good looking guy that Rorty, and also seems clever, perhaps more so than he actually is, it's better to be the other way round, like that bloody Tissier, he looks so idiotic that at least you're unlikely to be disappointed, eureka, Mr I'msobloodyintelligent has just thought of something that everyone will love, a country house hotel with golf, tennis and spa, on a mediaeval site in the Valois, just near Compiègne, this solution would, he thinks, have the advantage of getting away from it all that some of us have suggested, while remaining practical, yes, this solution seems to him a fantastic compromise, a coming together of everyone's wishes, yeah right, right, as if he hadn't thought of it ages ago, hadn't planned this pseudo-consultation and brilliant solution, great way to show us all who's boss, and to cap it all now he wants everyone to vote, who is for, ten hands go up, only Stoeffer is against, that Stoeffer is dying to punch Rorty's lights out, funny guy, reminds me of a bloke in my last company, a trade unionist, always handing out leaflets denouncing the activities of the management, I think he even took them to court for obstructionism or something, Stoeffer, used to be chief exec, apparently his company was pretty successful in the eighties but he lost almost everything when he sold it, during the Gulf War, lucky for him that he still handles the corporate communications for one of the company's biggest accounts, the Variphor labs, their communications director is an ex of his, he'll be all right as long as she's there, well, all right in a manner of speaking, I get the feeling that Rorty is planning a coup d'état via de Vals, if I do land the Vitalia account through Marc I'd better consolidate fast, otherwise I can wave goodbye to any kind of proper job, right, back to this away weekend, Compiègne sounds OK, let's hope we can have a bit of a laugh, golf, a gym and some tipsy little sluts in the evenings, remember that poor girl a couple of years ago at

Salt Consulting, what was her name again, an assistant project manager, Annie Sicart, yes, Annie Sicart, big arse, big tits, a bit thick, she ended up naked in the hotel pool, came back completely revved up, poor thing, and got fired three months later for professional inadequacy, Rorty is bringing the away-weekend discussion to a close and moving on to the next item on the agenda, in-house training, he's asking Tissier if he's made any progress on this, Tissier starts frowning like some kind of moody crooner, poor guy, he really thinks he's Dean Martin or James Bond or something, he's clearing his throat, he has noticed among the company's managerial staff, to which we all belong, a few people who could use some training in public speaking, Christ, this is all so laboured and pretentious, and anyway who is he to lecture us on communication, poor poor guy, his wife is leaving him, not bad if I remember rightly, country club type, organic free-range, amazing he ever landed her in fact, and that she has managed to hang on all this time, poor poor guy, as if he couldn't do with some public-speaking lessons himself, as well as a diet and some anti-dandruff shampoo, he's raining dandruff all over his collar, if I was a woman he'd score about two out of ten, hey, I hope I finally do my little pharmacist tonight, it's been going on a month now, I almost let it drop but she kept ringing me back, what does she look like again, I can see her slender thighs, and the boobs visible through her blouse but not her face, come on, concentrate, oh no, not a kaleidoscope of all my exes, start again, now I'm seeing

Meyer, wrong again, now Anne Brémont, that's the last straw, O Brémont, queen of the un-fucked, you're as big as a truck, Brémont, princess of the sexually frustrated, you look like a tuna in your sale-bought suit, my little pharmacist, I got in such a state last time I saw her, right, tonight, meal out and back home, I'll play my cards right, nightcap at mine, not very original I know, but it works ninety per cent of the time, what joy when I hear her fateful yes, or better still that moment's hesitation, overcome by a simple counter-argument, I'd give anything to live my whole life in that in-between moment, that prelude to paradise, infinite desire, the fabulous beauty of the female form, the dizziness of imminent union, the magic of the night, that's it, I'm hard, Casanova is back, long live the single life, what a mistake getting married just to divorce six months later, what nonsense, what a waste, any longer and I would have turned into Tissier, awful, I can just see him in his family house in the suburbs with his missus and the kids, same swimming trunks for over a decade, breakfasts already rancid with boredom, a whole life of habits and comforts, a whole life devoid of seduction and the firing of that divine spark in someone, someone who makes me feel so deliciously handsome, someone I'm endeavouring to conquer just so I can lose myself between her thighs . . .

3rd circle: Brémont

. . . I'm not sitting right, my back hurts, these chairs are so uncomfortable, and Tissier, dreary Tissier, still droning on about improving client rapport, rapport, what a ridiculous expression, this is like a 1980s management course, Tissier is so eighties himself, suggesting little pods of four or five people, role-play, videoed presentations, careful, rigorous analysis so that our little tics can be made crystal clear to each of us, the better to eradicate them, plus English lessons for the new staff who will be working with international clients, using the same model of role-play and videoed presentations, so Tissier is in charge of training now, why Tissier, he has no skills in the area, last year it was Françoise Clément-Dourville, she's the right person for the job, head of the legal and HR departments, why Tissier, that poor, square Tissier, he loves the sound of his own voice, his words all seem to dissolve into an annoying, incoherent mush, his forehead is glistening, his moustache trembling, he disgusts me, oh, now I'm all twitchy, I've had enough of sitting down, I'm hungry, my legs feel so heavy, Pujol is staring at me, what does that cut-rate Casanova want from me, I feel enormous, bovine, I wish I could find a boyfriend, but how, where should I go to meet one, and Tissier, Tissier still rambling on, yuk, not remotely sexy, Rorty is yawning openly, de Vals has pasted a happy grin on his face, Rorty is a handsome man, certainly, but I don't think I'd trust him, just the type to lead a double life, Tissier is talking about the importance of IT competence, all costs will be charged to the training budget, in accordance with the legal frameworks, ha, so he thinks he's a lawyer now, I feel sick, I ate too much again this morning, I'll never get a man if I keep stuffing myself like a turkey, I'm empty, so horribly empty, thank god for my girlfriends, I love chatting on the phone in the evenings, Lea and I were talking till 3am, her bloke had dumped her, I love it when my friends get dumped, we're rehearsing tonight, great, theatre club is so much fun at the moment, even better than last year, shame it's only gays and women, perhaps I should join a gym, Rorty is thanking Tissier and suggesting that we move on, after these pleasant digressions, to the more challenging issue, the mission with which he has been charged, which is to say corporate restructuring, I don't give a damn, I'm always winning new clients, I bring in at least six times my salary, expenses included, if they throw me out I'll have no trouble finding another job, at least I hope not, I'd better start thinking about my spiel in case Rorty questions me about the two new accounts and the delayed payments, remind him succinctly of the context with an emphasis on the main points of the company strategy that seduced the client, as for the delays I'll think of some excuse, I'm so dreadfully hungry, despite scoffing two Nutella blinis and two croissants for breakfast, I'm putting on more weight but at this point who cares, I'm thirty-six years old and bound to end up alone and childless, I may have attended a top university and been awarded a master's degree in applied psychology but I still feel as brainless as a butterfly, I live at a hundred miles an hour but without a compass, how I wish I'd been thirty in the seventies like my parents, everything was so much simpler for them, meeting, hanging out together for a while, getting a house, having kids, even if they did split up after years and years together, men today are such hard work, so reluctant to commit, and there are so many single women so much prettier than me, Barbara is celebrating her birthday at the Baron tonight, I'm bound to go home alone, watch out, the meat market is open, beauties first, then the rest, I hope I haven't caught anything, and from encounters that weren't even love affairs, that would be the last straw, men don't respect me, they despise me, out the door before their sperm has even cooled inside me, men don't love me and I don't love myself, I'm just a convenient hole, the fatty you grab at the end of the night when all the pretty ones have gone, and then discard like a used tissue, I feel like crying but I've got to concentrate, stay focused on this boring meeting, Rorty has moved on to the next item on the agenda, 'reception', reminding us that the reception is not merely the first point of call, it represents the company image, which is to say that the person on reception owes it to themselves to give a good impression of the company, to embody the corporate spirit in a manner of speaking, this role interfaces the inner and the outer and must therefore be undertaken with a total commitment to showing off the whole range of qualities likely to make us attractive to both clients and potential clients – qualities which include friendliness, grace, thoughtfulness, in short he cannot understand how a person so completely devoid of all these qualities could have been recruited and kept on, when there are hundreds of young students registered on agency books, in the interests of transparency he would like to inform the committee of the decision he has been forced to take in her regard, Françoise Clément-Dourville bursts in immediately, reminding him of the company's history, the two mergers which led to its integration into the group, reminds him that Christiane is one of the only survivors from the first merger, she's part of the furniture, she isn't well and she has a child to look after, you can't just play with people's lives like this, the company has a responsibility to its staff, Rorty tells her not to worry, he has made provision for a very substantial sum, which will see her through nicely, and anyway what's to say that this person won't find a better job elsewhere, yeah right, aged forty-five, that Rorty really is a bastard, Stoeffer cuts in suddenly, he agrees absolutely with Françoise, Christiane does her very badly paid work perfectly well, she is there to answer the phone not as a catwalk model, de Vals interrupts immediately, in an artificially neutral, objective tone, he'd like to describe his own experience, when he arrived for interview barely four months ago he must admit that he was surprised at the huge, spacey-looking lady on reception, he emphasises the huge, evoking Christiane's bulk with his hands, according to him it's an unavoidable if cruel decision, for the sake of the company and its client-facing image, a public-health measure one could say, Tissier looks slimy, ingratiating, Roussel pretends he hasn't heard, oh you brave men, Clément-Dourville and Stoeffer are shaking their heads sadly, they won't last long, those two, I need a man, nothing else really matters, perhaps I should go back to online dating, the last guy wasn't too bad, tall and thin, a graphic designer in advertising, an unprepossessing face like a retarded teenager and a lanky, unformed body, he left me several messages but I didn't reply, too nice, a bit insipid perhaps, but at this stage I should stop being so fussy, stop holding out for Prince Charming, hey, I wonder if Delphine is still with her trade unionist, at least he had a bit of character, too much perhaps, I couldn't do a trade unionist, they're so full of themselves, always busy protesting, demanding, attacking, I'd rather an executive, but hey, not someone massively busy with a mistress in every town, a man as ruthless professionally as he is gentle and attentive personally, physically I like them tall and thin, with blue eyes and a dimpled chin like Michael Douglas, continuing with his unilateral decisions Rorty is now presenting another of his dazzling propositions for internal restructuring, he's having quite a field day, he has worked out that certain services would cost the company less if they were out-sourced, he's thinking particularly of facilities, paying two people to twiddle their thumbs half the time is unthinkable, and would never happen in a company with an operating margin exceeding fifteen per cent, why not give them a lifelong allowance while we're at it, Françoise speaks up, sighing, she's got rings under her eyes, she's aged a lot over the last few months, she reminds me of mum's cousin who died from cancer after spending her life lurching from depression to depression, how old was I, eleven, eleven years old, when we went round there I used to be so freaked out by her skinniness, I remember at the time our family was always discussing Fritz Zorn's *Mars*, cancer as a consequence of neurosis, Françoise is trying desperately to defend herself, explaining that the previous management team, of which she was part, had taken that decision so as to better manage the fluctuations in supply needs, and although it's true that Philippe and Laurent do sometimes have slack moments, they work terribly hard, and never complain at working overtime during busy periods, the option of outsourcing facilities, which is what the company did before the two mergers, would not necessarily save money, Rorty interrupts the discussion to ask who is for the outsourcing of facilities, six hands go up, including mine, only Stoeffer, Françoise, Dominique Meyer and Alighieri are against, the outsourcing of the facilities service is therefore adopted, the two members of staff must be called for their preliminary interview, once inadequacies have been noted of course, Françoise will take care of it, Rorty is trusting her to manage this properly, I'm all twitchy again, my vagina is itching, it often does that at night, as I fall asleep, I'm hardly going to start scratching myself in the middle of a meeting, I should move more, take my body in hand, I could do body-sculpting classes twice a week and lose a stone in two months, like Aurelie, with her new figure she's already found a guy, she'd better keep at it if she doesn't want to lose him, I wouldn't mind going to the movies this weekend, I'll call Alexia, she wasn't doing anything Saturday night, mummy is having her knee operation tomorrow, I hope it goes smoothly, daddy is still in Germany, coming back tonight, Rorty has moved blithely on to the next item on the agenda, asking Françoise what progress she has made with EDM, Stoeffer asks what EDM means, Françoise tells him that it stands for Electronic Document Management, the management of the future, soon he won't have to deal with all this administrative paperwork, suppliers' invoices and client quotations, it will all be scanned and archived on the intranet so that it can be shared among all those involved, she explains that this initiative is in the process of being installed, the service providers have been working hard, the staff teams, on the other hand, are struggling, it's all so new, she looks at Tissier, the training plan must include a day dedicated to EDM for the entire management team, Rorty is stunned by this request, how can she request training for an initiative one is supposed to already understand, surely that's an absolute minimum for a project manager or an accountant, why not train them in handling figures while we're at it, I don't find Rorty's comment remotely amusing but I don't want to annoy him, what to do, to laugh or not to laugh, that is the question, I pretend I haven't heard, now Rorty is sniggering, obviously, and de Vals, what a nasty piece of work, always sucking up to Rorty, Roussel stretches languidly, too relaxed to trust that one Castaglione bursts out laughing, Castaglione is always bursting out laughing, she's looking at the rest of us, looking down from on high, I don't like her at all, she's a fake, calculating careerist, full of hate and contempt, her thirst for power is written all over her face, she looks down on me, to her I'm just a stupid little fatty, Tissier is wearing a grotesque, ugly smile, poor poor Tissier, I don't know what he does all day apart from checking his share prices online, I can't understand how he's got this far, he and Pujol are the biggest pair of incompetents I've come across in the whole of my working life, that crazy Castaglione and that scum de Vals at least are not completely immune to decent ideas, I'm still hungry, I'm not sitting right, if I uncross my legs my bum hurts even more, I hope I didn't catch Aids from that guy at Anne-So's party, I can still see myself sucking him off, he wasn't bad actually, but not very clean, and no one knew him, he'd come via a so-called friend who'd had to cancel at the last minute, and to top it off he gave me a fake phone number, Rorty is on to the accounting now, kicking off by lecturing Françoise Clément-Dourville about some unpaid invoices, how is it that certain managers are able to organise not only signed order forms from their clients but also payment in advance, whereas others wait until the work is completed before claiming their fees, usually revised downwards, not to mention all the outstanding payments, which absolutely must be collected, what is the financial director doing to recover these monies, what are the relevant managers doing, I must stop drinking like a fish every night, I get completely out of control, anything can happen, and does, this morning my forehead was itching, could be the first symptoms, no, come on, a little scratching is hardly Kaposi's sarcoma, but I could have caught it anyway, being so free with my body, giving it to just about anyone, I got such a shock when I read Guibert's *Cytomegalovirus*, especially that scene where he describes the Columbian mafia gouging out the eyes of local teenagers, organ trading, organised crime, cancer, aids, dehumanised inner cities where organised crime and prostitution reign, it's all inhuman, so terribly inhuman, I think of Guibert and my list of nameless lovers flashes before my eyes like some kind of deadly dance, no, I must stop thinking like this, I don't have Aids, at least I hope not, oh, that's funny, when I look at Tissier I calm down, yes, strange, the sight of Tissier reassures me, he's so normal, so ordinary, just like the mundane, two-dimensional life he embodies, the life of peaceful, eternal France, of smiling villagers and green valleys, apparently he's in the middle of a divorce, so what, I still imagine him with his missus and his little family, very fifties, very provincial, three

33

kids and a Labrador, the whole family must wait for him every evening, for him, the head of the family, the head of that same family I would so love to create with this man I am bound never to meet . . .

4th circle: Tissier

. . . I do hope the court dismisses the case and awards me joint custody, after all she's the one who wants to leave, she's the one demanding 4500€ alimony every month, the hearing is on Thursday, let's hope I don't lose custody of the kids, let's hope I don't have to pay those 4500€ for the rest of my life, Rorty is looking at me strangely, I don't know what he wants but I know it's nothing good, the world of work is becoming tougher and tougher, this isn't the time to get myself fired, Sebbag and Blanchet still haven't found work, I'm no better off than them, maybe even a little older, my haemorrhoids are still bothering me, I'm tired, I'd like to lie down, Dr Watz's pills no longer have the slightest effect, I'm bleeding constantly, it's becoming quite intolerable, I'll have to have an operation, there's no other option, as if I didn't have enough on my plate already, apparently it's horribly painful, agony whenever you sit down, for a whole month – great for someone who spends their life in meetings, and then there's the hypotension, 230/150 at my last check-up, I'll have to take beta blockers, Rorty's interrogating Anne-Laure Brémont now, asking her to explain herself regarding the delayed CRAPIF payment, she was supposed to have chased up all the outstanding invoices last week, poor Brémont is stuttering, talking rubbish, there was Easter weekend, she had spoken to the client on the phone, he had agreed her quotation in principle but her teams hadn't warned her of the payment delay, she wasn't told of the problem in time, Laure who manages the account has just gone on maternity leave, there was an agreement in principle, it will all be formalised imminently, an agreement in principle on which quotation bellows Rorty, his splutter lit up, as if to emphasise his fury, in the ray of sunshine filling half the room, here we go, she bursts into tears, Rorty looks delighted with himself, as for me I have to admit I'm not averse to seeing her grilled like this, why deny oneself the petty pleasures of corporate life, Rorty is saying yet again, Rorty is quite aware that he's repeating himself and will not be doing so again, because he's had enough of repeating things, from now on every quotation must be approved by the supervisory committee that has been in place since February, a committee consisting of Arnaud, Sophie and himself, every financial transaction absolutely must be approved by this authority, which will take into account not only the obvious issue of the time spent on the project but also the quality of service and the type of documents to be produced, each manager is duty-bound to manage his or her client's budget efficiently and to make sure close track is kept of both revenue and expenses, Rorty is moving on to the next item on the agenda, the transfer of the Unilife and Brevitis accounts from Stoeffer's to de Vals's team, you know what, if Stoeffer starts losing his existing accounts he won't have much left, he's been coming into the office less and less recently, though he's not on secondment as far as I know, Stoeffer seems resigned, well, resigned in a manner of speaking, his level of resignation actually depends on his alcohol levels, poor guy, his time will soon be up, though Rorty should definitely watch out for physical violence, the man is raving mad, capable of anything, apparently he spent time in prison in the late seventies, for his participation in an anarcho-socialist movement related to the Red Brigades, the seventies, the thirty-year boom, that blessed time when you could quit your job and find another paid twice as much the next day, and have sex without being taken to court, our era is quite tragic, so morose, so tough, such hard work, the struggle to find a job, to keep it, or find another if you lose it, domestic violence, demanding women who spend their lives pointing out your failings and making you feel like a loser, an immature, neurotic loser, poor Stoeffer, Rorty will force him to leave, definitely, Stoeffer could punch him in the face, he could set the best lawyer in Paris on him at the industrial tribunal, it wouldn't change a thing, my god, let's hope they're not planning to fire me, let's hope I'm still on staff in a year, or two or three or four, how am I going to afford alimony, private school for the kids, holidays at Club Med, rent for my new flat while we sell the old one, Rorty's jesting now that we're moving on to a contentious subject, a subject that caused much debate at our last strategic committee meeting, yes, you guessed it, the abolition of the famous thirteenth-month bonus, we have prevaricated for long enough and now we must act, a small sacrifice by the staff will greatly advantage the corporation, we're all pretty well paid, these routine perks are killing the economy, Françoise Clément-Dourville looks devastated, she has always opposed this, it's illegal, you can't cancel established perks, Rorty replies that you certainly can do it, legally, all the more so because it's nothing, not even a written agreement, just a habit one can simply shed in the interests of streamlining, the staff can of course go to court if they want but I fear they may be dismissed before their case is even heard, concludes Rorty slowly and cynically, courts, courts, I feel as if that's the only word I hear, all day long, what with the divorce, that charity suing me for not helping a person in danger because some bloody homeless guy snuffed it on my doorstep, and crazy Julia accusing me of sexual harassment, that will teach me to sleep with subordinates, she'll squeeze the maximum possible damages out of me, I can't take any more, I'm at the end of my tether, what have I done to deserve this hell, all I want is a bit of peace but my life is becoming more and more chaotic, from an objective point of view I had all you need to be happy, excellent qualifications, robust health, a pretty wife, two wonderful children, well-connected friends, a senior job in a prestigious company, and yet everything is falling apart around me, Pierre-Yves says I must have bad karma, must have done wrong in a former life, no, seriously, I've had enough, in any case if my troubles continue to multiply I'll no longer be able to cope and I'll leave, like those missing men who suddenly abandon their work, their family, their home, leaving no address, sometimes even taking on a new identity to avoid being found, I'll go to Quebec, start over with a strong, pretty young Canadian girl, teach management in a French college, I'll have an apartment in Montreal, a house in the Laurentides and a convertible Buick, my new friends will be professors with attractive young students in tow, like in *The Decline of the American Empire,* maybe it's not such a crazy idea, I'm forty-nine and there's nothing to stop me starting over, in the meantime I'm working over twelve hours a day just to pay the lawyers and the family overheads, there's no sign of anything better on the horizon and I'm nervous about this court case, I hope they'll at least not take my kids away, that bitch is capable of anything, perjury, to think she looks as if butter wouldn't melt in her mouth, poor Chantal, so sensitive, so fragile, etc etc, my wife is leaving me and my mistress has taken it into her head to magic up a harassment case, if only I'd known, the bitch had it all worked out in advance, even planting colleagues in the restaurant so there would be witnesses, and the whole time Chantal was having it off with her karate coach, what's worse I introduced them, at that corporate communications prize-giving ceremony, I should never have trusted that short little slimeball, too polite to be honest, yes, I remember now, he was staring at her as if he wanted to eat her up, a karate black belt fourth dan, he'd be able to hit me four times before I'd landed a single punch, Rorty is still extolling the benefits of austerity, ouch, my haemorrhoids, shooting pain whenever I move an inch, it's unbearable, and the blood pressure is worrying, the doctor was categorical, I've got to lose weight, go on a diet, take exercise, I've never been much of a sportsman, it'll be hard, if I'm going to be reduced to dry bread and water I might as well throw in the towel, Chantal with a karate instructor and Julia using our unequal relationship to attack me in court, tragic, I had a wife and a mistress and now I find myself with two court cases on the go, ouch, the bastards are torturing me again, I'm not sitting right, these chairs aren't designed for the fat and veinally challenged, Rorty clearly doesn't have any of these problems, Rorty is svelte and athletic, Rorty hates excess weight, he's only trying to maintain employment without sacrificing company profit, you have to find the right balance of work and capital said Karl, isn't that right Pierre-Henri, he looks at me knowingly, I smile back, a bit forced perhaps, my mouth frozen in an ape-like grimace, I can't drop the smile, Rorty notices everything, he's remembering that I did a history thesis on the dissemination of revolutionary ideas in the work of Marx and Proudhon, when he first started he called me in and I must have mentioned it, Marx and Proudhon, the feuding brothers of socialism, the first attack came from Proudhon in *Philosophy of Poverty*, if I remember rightly he laid into his era's bour-geois spiritualism as much as into dialectical materialism,

Marx immediately responded with his *Poverty of Philosophy,* mum and dad attended my Viva, I got a first, they were so proud, twenty-five years ago already, a happy time, I was still a free man, not yet crippled by debts and legal cases, I no longer read, don't have the time, what was the last one, oh yes, *The Da Vinci Code,* almost a year ago, a good, intelligent, esoteric thriller, no, not quite a year, it was during the Christmas holidays, five months then, but since that nothing, I can't even seem to finish that essay on the end of humanism and the omnipotence of genetics, though it's a fascinating subject, intelligent matter, prosthetics, genetically modified landscapes, what's it called again, not *From the Closed World to the Infinite Universe,* nor *Chaos and Harmony,* much less *The Selfish Gene,* oh well, it'll come back to me, anyway, for some time now man has been falling off his pedestal and my problems have been multiplying at the speed of light, how have I managed to go this far astray, how did the enthusiastic, hopeful young graduate become this poor stressed-out guy, battered by life, perfect candidate for a heart attack, I can hear my tired heart beating, my overloaded veins itch and great crowds of insoluble problems keep charging around my brain, blast, I forgot to take my vein tonics again this morning, Chantal was being so awful, she blew in without warning, and I just know that guy was waiting for her on the doorstep, Rorty is asking Castaglione how she's getting on with the next HR seminar, he seems quite hypnotised by the woman, she is certainly formidable,

Chantal times ten, capable of anything to get what she wants, I can tell she despises me, no surprise there, I am no use to her, she's playing Rorty's game by ostentatiously listing the name and title of every invitee, there'll even be a big shot from the Economic and Social Council, an expert in ageing and the consequences of demographic reversal on the working population pyramid, a vast subject agrees Rorty, no, I must be dreaming, he who is constantly banging on about new blood, interns and forced early retirement for staff in their fifties, not only does he dare agree, he even looks devastated, disgusted by the naughty companies that dismiss experienced and competent staff, Rorty congratulates Sophie Castaglione once again, in a field where human relationships are so important one cannot live in isolation, these breakfast briefings she organises with such enthusiasm are becoming a real laboratory of entrepreneurship, why not an artistic avant garde while we're at it, that Castaglione is a real Marquise de Merteuil, she doesn't bring in any revenue and works two hours a day but she has an incredible influence on Rorty, I think deep down he's scared of her, she really is formidable, International HQ knew exactly what they were doing parachuting her in, she's already given poor old Sebbag and Blanchet the push and she's not going to stop there, she's a schemer, a cold-blooded assassin, I don't like the way she looks down at me, what contempt in her eyes, to her I am Tissier the ugly, the potbellied, Tissier the company cockroach, it's been so long since anyone looked at me with

love, I know I'm no longer very appealing, I've put on a lot of
weight, sailed merrily past the fourteen stone mark, not great
for someone of five foot seven, to think that at twenty I
weighed ten stone soaking wet, but is that worthy of such
contempt, my haemorrhoids are causing me unbearable pain,
I'm going to explode, scatter my guts and entrails all over
the room, Rorty is asking each manager to cultivate client
relationships using not only brains but soul, don't hesitate
to surprise your clients by inviting them, for example, to
contemporary art exhibitions, themed days, festivals and
who knows what all, be prepared to use your weekends and
TOIL, the word toil seems to entertain Rorty greatly, France
is resting, she mustn't be woken, we're the country where
people work least and they have to create iniquitous laws on
top, well, he's forgotten to mention that we also have one of
the world's highest rates of productivity per hour, not that
I'm about to contradict him, here we go, he's denouncing the
culture of leisure and idleness in which France is bogged
down, he prefers the American model, employment legislation
is much less restrictive there, and the economy vastly more
dynamic, he sniggers, it's not by working a thirty-five-hour
week that America has got to where it is, Castaglione nods,
de Vals mentions Japan, he worked there for four years, their
legislation is extremely favourable to entrepreneurs and
risk-takers, that horrid little careerist grabs the opportunity to
flatter Rorty by telling him that one day his voice will be heard,
that the history of ideas as of economics is cyclical, everyone

starts putting their tuppence worth in, their thoughts, their position on this reduction of working hours, ouch, haemorrhoids again, I must be bleeding, I'll have a look later, in the lav, it's agony, sometimes I'm in so much pain I want to kill myself . . .

5th circle: Stoeffer

Howling Munch mouth, ruined Baconesque face, exploding head à la Di Rosa, bones collapsing, sphincters releasing, the whole lot swimming in blood and piss, it would be good, it would be fair, that scum deserves no less, scum, scum, the man is scum, no respect, no compassion, nothing, obvious what side he'd have been on in the camps, scum, such scum, and that poor Anne-Laure Brémont, and the pathetic posturing of the brainstorming lunches, what a sight, the company is growing and blossoming from the foulest dung, that scum lulling us with his pompous, vacuous speeches on change and evolution, nothing can ever be taken for granted, we can always do better, beat our own records, Lindbergh would never have accomplished his voyage if he hadn't had the strength to keep awake through extreme exhaustion, and the best scientific inventions, and the best works of art, and the best of human accomplishment, all born of this incredible determination to free oneself from the grip of habit and convention, lies, arrogance and bluffing galore, he calls this the anthropology of change, the poor girl is in tears, my lungs are burning up, I'm going to cough, three packs a day, good score, marvellous score my dear Richard, you're beating your own record, smoking kills, smoking reduces fertility, smoking makes you impotent, smoking causes serious illness, poor bloody idiots, try as you may to avoid smoker's cancer you can never force a radioactive cloud to stop at your borders or asbestos fibres to shrink back from your lungs, or lead, or mercury, or toxic fumes from polytetrafluoroethylene-coated frying pans, nor can you make pesticides, the allergenic and carcinogenic particles in composite materials, solvents, molecules of dichlorodi-phenyltrichlorethane, polychlorinated biphenyls, phthalate flame retardants or the perfluoric acid detected in the blood of thirty-nine British MPs sidestep you, you, just because you don't want to die of cancer, nor will all the deadly, invisible pollutants in the water, the air and the earth live their lives around you, leaving you safe, landing on the neighbours, or abroad, who cares as long as it's not on you, have some more tofu, my dear Richard, the advent of the protoplasmic company, yeah right, protoplasmic my arse, all he wants is to decrease costs to get the highest possible dividends for the shareholders, I saw what they were like when they bought me out, making the newest staff redundant and overloading the rest, reduction of the wage bill, breaking points, breakdowns, the rest is just marketing, publicity and the seduction of imbeciles, and me, and us, and the employees, what will become of them in this unspeakable decluttering, handsome Rorty, so good-looking, just asking to be pulverised, face down in the bog, ear nailed to the wall, nose up de Vals' arse, balls in a juicer, they're taking another two accounts from me, I'll soon be flushed out like a turd, I can feel it coming, not the time to screw up, they're lying in wait, suspension, etc etc, how I'd love to throw myself on that scum Rorty, a punch first to make him stagger, knock him down and straddle him, rain blows on his nose, his mouth, his head, what delight imagining his little face disfigured and bleeding, would I manage to knock him down, who knows, it's been a long time since those judo trophies, three packs of fags and four big whiskies a day do take their toll, farewell to physical stamina, speed, breath, energy . . . strangling is the only solution, if I can keep hold of him he'll be fucked, but he might manage some low blows before I find a firm grip, the fucker is lean, toned and vicious, such contempt in his eyes, his posture, his words, to think that he's constantly singing his own praises to the press, presenting himself as an ardent defender of human rights, sustainable development and social dialogue, the media is heaving with interviews with this scum, lecturing us on public spirit when he behaves like a pig, a sordid, despicable pig, if I hadn't been so high up I'd have been a trade unionist, just for the pleasure of pissing him off, attacking him in the courts, shoving his vileness in his face without being fired, would have been a trade unionist so I was protected, untouchable, hated by the management and despised by my own colleagues, banned from pay rises, left out of promotions, a slave to social rights, representing justice in a lawless universe, the next step, I know it, he'll call me into his office and try to grill me on how I see myself in the company in a few years time, offer me some useless agreement like keep your account, and I do still have one account thank god, and become a kind of freelance consultant, you'll see, it'll be much better for everyone, and I'll say fuck you, out of the question, I'm an employee of this goddamn company that I created nearly twenty years ago, then they'll offer me a settlement, one year, perhaps two, I'll tell them to fuck themselves again, at my age there's no question of making a deal, I'll get my lawyer onto them, they'll try to intimidate me, I'll take them to the industrial tribunal which will give me a year and a half, maximum two years' redundancy, in short, best to avoid any mistakes, it's a question of life and death for me, for us, I'm hardly alone in all this, Judith, the restaurant, if it bombs I can already see the bank, the taxman, all that hassle galloping towards us, we've got into quite some debt with this business, a Mexican restaurant, not what you'd call a sure bet exactly, a nightmare in fact, six months to persuade that bloody banker, six months of waiting, stress and vexation to get this lousy project up and running, no point in going bankrupt from a mis-negotiated redundancy, I'm too old to think a couple can live on love and water, after the tribunal we could always go to appeal, Krantz was saying they're much more generous with employees who'd struggle to find a new job, at fifty I should do well on that score at least, he gave the example of that fifty-five-year-old employee fired without a real and proper reason, his massive public-works company forced to compensate right up to retirement, justice is sometimes done in this country, to think that twenty years ago I found all this unemployment and retirement stuff amusing, what an arrogant fool, success addles your brain, failure makes you aware of your limitations, the eighties, so long ago, so unreal, did I really have my hour of glory or was it all an illusion, a dream designed to trick me, the eighties, Stoeffer the trailblazer, the guru of corporate communications, all the prizes, the girls falling like flies, the clubs – Le Palais, Les Bains – models, actresses, interns, all as gorgeous as they were high, Deauville, all vanished now, will life seem as brief and time as spiteful, the last time I went to a club it was awful, suffocating, the horrible feeling of being a sugar daddy, no, not even that, an old bastard, and afterwards the buzzing ears and the cold sweats, I've put on more weight since, must stop smoking and drinking like this, the doctor has warned me, but after all, it would hardly be a great loss to society, I lost everything when I sold Starcorp, lost myself by staking my whole career on a hypothetical success, living is learning to lose said some fashionable philosopher in the eighties, who was it, Cioran I think, yes, Cioran, that saying is so true, invented for me, made to measure, and what do you know he's back on his hobby horse, going on about endings, knowing how to break with one's habits, his vision of the world, the best scientists knew how to shake off the old paradigms so as to adopt new ones, this scum reciting his bible, learnt by heart from god knows what manual of staff development, what vile gibberish, when I was company director I never used this kind of brainwashing, just tried to get them to understand their role at the heart of the collective, and did my best to make it all go as well as possible but look at this, such dumbing down, it's disgusting, ah, here we go, he's on to holism now, everything is contained in everything and each element is reflected in the whole which reflects each of its elements, if one single element falters the whole is affected, can no longer progress, to revive the whole, the diseased part must be cut out, eradicated, the fucking Nazi, what revolting nonsense, justifying his hatefulness with a hotchpotch of the Californian new age, despite the respect I have for the Palo Alto crew, Huxley, Watzlawick, Bateson, etc, I don't swallow, never have swallowed this HR mysticism, we're fed that crap in order to obscure our real condition – caged rats, that's what we are, rats desperately seeking a way out, except there is no way out, or only death, that's the way out, and the worst thing is that the others seem to be swallowing this idiocy, de Vals looks totally entranced by the big boss, de Vals, what a noxious piece of work, prototype of the devoted, dynamic manager, capable of all kinds of baseness to achieve his ends, as for Tissier, he'd better watch out or his number'll be up, the slightest wrong step and bosh, and he's in the middle of a filthy divorce, poor guy, Françoise looks completely shattered, as well she might, what with her personal problems, her husband dying, I should have lunch with her more often, at least in that regard I'm not doing too badly, Judith is on great form, my ex too, I'm lucky with her, our daughter is lovely, and her new boyfriend, an architecture student, nice boy, someone wholesome at last, balanced, not like all these cockroaches, look at Pujol greedily lapping up the big man's words, pitiful swell that he is, two-faced bastard if ever there was one, to think that I have to endure this spectacle every day that God brings – well, God in a manner of speaking, even the faithful have more and more trouble believing such a wacky, kitsch notion, this is the only place where one still has to prostrate oneself before the sole words of the supreme being, the divine charisma of the Word incarnate, these strategy committees are grotesque farces to the glory of the führer, the duce, the caudillo, the company is totalitarian, totalitarian in its rituals, its foundations, its organisational chart, these imbeciles wouldn't understand even if I explained, they have such a sense of being within their rights, oh that dreadful speech he gave to Sebbag and Blanchet, yes, I know you understand boys, I've nothing against you personally boys, it's not my fault, it's the corporation, the shareholders in fact, they're asking for more than I can give boys, we're too numerous and too well paid, I have to make a choice, every choice is unfair, unfair of course but I have to take a decision, we're all in the same boat, you're still young, you'll find new jobs, we can talk again, my door is always open, what scum, I'll kill him one day, no, not kill him just hurt him, accidentally poke out his eye or break his nose, no, not hurt him, just humiliate him, lock him in an office after having made him drink castor oil and come back with all the employees, no, humiliation is too gentle for such a cockroach, Nico and Charly are coming over tonight, I'll make them one hell of a Columbian whisky cocktail, and what if I stopped drugging myself, tomorrow, the healthy life, jogging in the woods every morning, the birds, the smell of greenery, oxygen, joining a health club and eating organic, oh god, that must be so bloody boring, I'd rather die immediately, no, perhaps I could re-qualify, ten more years of retirement contributions to make, if they fire me I'll still have to work, but what could I do, gardener, hey, why not a gardener, they don't seem stressed, but how much are they paid, probably not much more than the minimum wage, how would I live, no, teacher at a private school, but then, who knows if they'd take me, I've nothing, no diploma, no institutional legitimacy, de Vals is staring at me, who does he think he is, looking at me like that, turkey brain, little Rorty-grovelling bastard, hold me back or I'll be at his throat, I can already see myself smashing his arterial windpipe, only thing is, if you wiped him out there'd be a hundred, a thousand others, all as dynamic, devoted, proactive and perfect as the content of a small ad in the recruitment section of a management journal, the other roach is still lecturing us on evolution – apathy and excess weight are the greatest enemies of evolution, besides, look at the dinosaurs, man is made for overtaking, OK, philosophy, Rorty is giving us a philosophy lesson, I could puke, I think I'm going to be sick right here, mid-meeting, in front of them all, at least it would bring this sad spectacle to an end, it's obscene, someone stop him, what's more these imbeciles actually look interested, listening properly, attentively, that crazy Castaglione stroking her chin and eyeing him greedily, what voracity, the woman is a real cunt on legs, and that weird Pujol nodding idiotically, Tissier taking notes like a good boy, Roussel staring at Rorty sarcastically, not a good way up the ladder my friend, poor guy, to think that he was taken on to improve creative standards and the only thing he's been asked to do is get rid of the dead wood from his teams, resource shortage here, redundancy settlement there, Meyer's still got that aloof look on her face, only that block-head Alighieri seems not to give the remotest shit, he's not too bad, that boy, likewise certain to annoy Il Duce, he'll be summoned before too long, the worst of all scum that Rorty, my first impression of him was bad and first impressions are always right, scum, I could arrange for contract killers to wait for him at the front door of the office, take him into the countryside and kill him after having methodically made him suffer, or, better still, shoot him like a dog, a quick gunshot and out of there full of pride and contempt, nothing, just a bang in the silence, when grandpa took me out hunting the first thing that disturbed me was the ease with which life can be taken, a simple squeeze of the finger and it's over, nothing left but this small, still-warm, already inert thing . . .

6th circle: De Vals

. . . trim and muscular, sure, but hair already greying at the temples, and lines creeping onto his brow, death's empire never stops gaining ground, everywhere, day after day, what will he be like in twenty years, thirty, forty, how will he die, in an aeroplane crash or a nursing home, I can just imagine him in a dressing gown wandering the halls of some luxury institution, The Lilacs or The Gladioli, with Cezanne prints on the walls and lots of maids hoovering, that crazy Castaglione is laying it on so thick with her breakfast briefings, I can't understand how she's got this far considering what new business she brings in, must be her contacts or her arse, perhaps both, Rorty is watching her with suspicious intensity, what does he see in that lunatic, with her sickly grey pallor, ageing model's figure and lugubrious voice, she'd terrify me, and what's more she's as mean as a bag of snakes, Rorty is definitely courting her, this endless discussion of the breakfast briefings is absurd, I've got fewer wrinkles than him, not forty yet, the youngest person here, pick things up in a flash, I'm an exceptional man, ha, I've just glimpsed the make of his suit, bit of a let-down, I would have expected better, so he's actually a bit cheap, this Rorty, I really wouldn't be a bad replacement, go on Rorty, have a heart attack, or cancer, or bird flu, whatever, just make sure they need to find you a successor, for now though, unfortunately, he seems in perfect health, always tanned, toned, not exactly the ideal candidate for a heart attack, not like Tissier and Stoeffer, such wrecks, they seem to be confusing the firm with a hospice, I'd get them out on early retirement, I would, off you go chaps, but maybe there's still hope with Rorty, apparently he takes a lot of uppers, Sandrine came across him early one morning with masses of pills on his desk, he was horrified to see her, come on Rorty, just a little overdose, if that happened I'd phone Barco who'd appoint me immediately, hopefully he'd still be President of the group, how soon is Rorty likely to snuff it, ten, fifteen years, maybe more, maybe less, I'll have to be patient, they'd soon see that compared to me Rorty was a soft, lethargic leftist, I'd phone mum, she'd be so happy, so proud, I am cut out for great things and I'll get rid of the lot of you, first things first, deal with that crazy Castaglione, she has good international contacts, her address book is probably far better than mine, I'd have to watch out for her, Rorty, hand-some Rorty, his Wasp side really turns me on, I wouldn't mind screwing him in the first-floor loos, I'd make him wear a big frizzy blonde wig and have him suck me off, call him my pretty little doll, beat him up and chuck him out like a scuzzy tissue, bloody arrogant playboy, that would be so funny, I wonder, is he better looking than me, I'm not sure, I looked pretty good in the mirror this morning, pretty good, especially with tensed pecs and biceps, ten hours of weights a week soon produces results, he's muscular too but less so, much less than me, taller but less muscular, me Tarzan, you Jane, to think that every one of them thinks I'm engaged, settled, monogamous, they should have seen me last night at the Vit Club, with that group of face-lifted, boob-jobbed English slappers, they reminded me of fat, over-excited turkeys, let's hope the silly bitches didn't give me anything, or that big pierced guy from last weekend at Deeper, that's it, my heart's thumping, I'm trembling, anxious, these fucking diseases really freak me out, I'd better not have a panic attack, where are my pills, in the office, I suppose I could always step out for a moment, come on, think about something else, focus on Rorty, corporate fatcat through and through, he's a great entertainer basically, my pretty little doll, can't remember which evening it was that I jerked off to thoughts of you, picking mushrooms in your pyjamas, in a clearing, I was your Prince Charming and had to fight my way through brambles and bushes to reach you and after, what delight to pull down your pyjamas and penetrate you while squeezing my hands tight around your neck, you resisted like a brave warrior but I was so much stronger than you, it was great, to think that you trust me implicitly, to think that you consider me your right-hand man, of course I play my part well, and I also work hard, the best sales, the biggest turnover, my team has the best productivity ratio and all the year's biggest accounts, manufacturing, leisure and general interest campaigns, and it

57

was me who won them, I've got you by the goatee, little Rorty, yes, business success tends to hinge on the basic equations, my god Clément-Dourville is such a sad, sad woman, Rorty is bullying her again, telling her that the restructuring of the company is forcing him to reconceptualise the use of space, he has worked it all out with an interiors architect, for now this should be kept quiet but the decision has been taken, our company will henceforth be a transparent, open space, which will mean knocking down partitions, opening up, and the perfect solution – he would even say the only solution, having looked at the issue from every possible angle – is to move the legal and financial department, which currently occupies most of the third floor, down to the ground floor, formerly home to the facilities service which is now to be outsourced, he informs her of all this without drawing breath, she replies in a flat, bitter voice that firstly, she can't see how her department, which unless she is very much mistaken consists of about ten staff, can be expected to function in a box which was already tight for two, and may she remind him, while she's at it, that work legislation gives each member of staff the right to a minimum of fifteen square metres in a private office or seven open plan, secondly she would have appreciated Rorty taking this kind of decision after consultation with the workers' council and the staff in question, dear god that woman is ugly and unlikeable, she's old, her wrinkles are bad for the company image, when I bring clients to the office I always hate them bumping into her, when I've gone to such lengths to impress them with the youth and beauty of my team, at least I was able to recruit my team myself, I'd boot all these losers out on early retirement, I would, go on, be off with you, I wonder how Rorty will respond, ah, I see, he's going for the consensual Social Democrat approach, unless I am very much mistaken it's the Chief Executive who runs the company, the staff representative bodies will of course be consulted, in accordance with the law, but he would like to remind her that the workers' council is in any case advisory in nature, as for the supposed lack of space, the architect has planned a most ingenious office layout, the spaces will overlap with one another to create the impression of the missing square metres, the illusion of missing metres in thirty square metres, that would be something, Clément-Dourville is sighing, shaking her head, looking at Stoeffer, the two linch-pins of the company, linchpins my arse, to me they're more like clapped-out furniture, scruffy old tables, chairs, sofas or whatever, time to throw them out, chuck them on the skip, those two are made for each other, if I was Rorty I'd be managing the generational renewal with a bit more guts, this funereal atmosphere does my head in, reminds me of those endless lunches at home with the extended family, old uncles, old aunts, old cousins from Normandy, all old, all fat, pickled in prune liqueur and decked out in their farming medals, hideous, I was the black sheep of the family, the token intellectual slapped down for a laugh, wretched fat peasants, awful provincial snobs, I was always getting beaten up at school, I was the smallest, the scrawniest, a bit soft perhaps, country kids are such lumps, stupid, dirty and nasty, a vile mob living on borrowed time till the next natural disaster, bring on the greenhouse effect, chemical pollution, climate change, sustainable development be damned, and social dialogue and all that humanist bollocks, Rorty is looking all professorial, he's cooking up one of those monologues he's so good at, to think that he's writing a book on organisational change, some mishmash of philosophy, anthropology and management-speak, go on then, sweet Rorty, tell us about change, mutations, Darwinism, the importance of rediscovering one's taste for new targets and for challenge, no, he's starting more humbly today, looking down, deferential, my dear Françoise, if you are expecting me not to change anything in this company and to let things remain as they are then you're in for a surprise, and in fact I have never hidden my desire to move things forward, my dear Françoise here, my dear Françoise there, it's true that this must be a bitter pill to swallow for the poor woman, I feel for her, me who hates compassion, I'm with Nietzsche, compassion is a despicable emotion, the civilised lamb reproaches the eagle for being an eagle and therefore eating him, and therefore being bad, while he, the lamb, is good because he doesn't eat the eagle, which is how the morality of slaves, the morality of compassion becomes the universal law, one of Nietzsche's greatest ideas, *On the Genealogy of Morals,* kept it by my bed when I was twenty, poignant memories of Brasillach's *Sept*

Couleurs, Gide's *Fruits of the Earth,* and dear Drieu's *Feu follet* and *Reveuse bourgeoisie,* not to mention Barrès, Morand, Papus, Papus was such a revelation, a wake-up call to the world of the spirit, and then Guénon and his *Reign of Quantity,* and *Man and His Becoming According to the Vedanta,* and *Symbolism of the Cross,* and then Bataille's great fusion of the mystical and the erotic, the slave is telling Rorty that it's not a question of defending the status quo or opposing all change, just of behaving with a bit more sense – shoving a whole department into a cubbyhole is an aberration, pure and simple, she's asking Rorty to put himself in his employees' shoes, you can't cram staff in like animals, you can't play with their lives and personal space as if these were unimportant details, some of them have worked for the company for ten, twenty years and are feeling increasingly insecure, on his last annual visit the company doctor noted that a vast and increasing proportion of the company's staff were on anti-depressants, he has written a report which he is going to file with a joint committee responsible for studying health at branch level, poor poor slave, your compassionate views are so old fashioned, your life expectancy is almost zero, tomorrow's companies will be flawless, tough and without mercy, the weak, the ugly, the fat, the old, the slow and the stupid will have no place in them, Rorty is delighted that the company doctor is taking such care and that the joint committees are discussing issues as compelling as physical and mental health at work, but the change must be implemented, it's an urgent necessity, without change there will be no company, and therefore no employment, if some of our colleagues are so concerned with their nerves why don't they work for the state, although it does seem that the public sector is slowly discovering the virtues of productivity and competition, I can tell you honestly, he continues, that I would be quite happy for your staff to come and see me whenever they want, my door is open and we can discuss these things amicably, personally, and I will clear up their fears, or vice versa perhaps, Rorty smiles, his teeth are not a spotless white, disappointing, I would have expected better from him, my last appointment with the hygienist was a month ago, Dr Olmek's new treatment is extremely effective, such a thrill to finally be able to smile with confidence, that woman's teeth really are disgusting, I'd blow my brains out if I was her, quick, easy, I can't imagine being fifty, much less sixty, having said that if I carry on being so careless I'll never get old, I could already be infected, unaware that I haven't long to live, I don't care, I won't go for an HIV test, I don't want to know, I'm going to the Body Club tonight, two hours of weights and an hour in the sauna and steam room, and then I'll meet Christophe and Gilles at Vit's, last year I met the XLT communications director there, if this lot only knew how I recruit my clients, ha, but the method doesn't matter, the important thing is to win the account, and therefore the cash, that's the law, that's my law, make a shitload of cash so I can stay this handsome for as long as possible and have it off with whoever I want, roar around in my convertible when I feel like it, buy studio apartments and let them out to morons and sluts that I can probably screw as well, and then one day be able to stop work and live like a sultan, surrounded by slaves with sexy, athletic bodies, but for that to happen I'd better take over from this bloody Rorty, or his equivalent in some other corporation, one thing is for sure, my future is in the international market, at group level, perhaps I should get closer to Castaglione, make her an ally, I could move in on her contacts, the only thing is I don't know her, I know nothing of her life, oh yes, yes I do, I know something, something which is the most important thing in the world to her, something she looks after, houses, feeds and sometimes brings in to work, Jean-Christophe I think his name is, that French bulldog she always trails around, horrible beast, always slobbering, snoring or farting, astonishing for such a haughty ice-queen, completely nuts over it, yes, that's it, that's the flaw, I'll have to go via the dog to get closer to her, get myself to the pet shop pronto and buy a French bulldog, a puppy three or four months old, they sleep for more than twelve hours a day apparently, you just have to take them out for one little walk, I could always leave it on the balcony in the day time, it could chase the pigeons, and when I go on holiday or away on business I'll put it in some kind of kennel, a French bulldog, now there's a good idea, we'll hit it off with each other through our dogs, it's a dead cert, and when we're friends maybe she'll let me into her network, what a great idea, not easy to come up with that one, ha,

I'm so smart, not wanting to boast but I am cunning, very cunning, one of the warrior's most important qualities according to Clausewitz, cunning and the art of attacking the enemy in the most unexpected way, hers is a male, I'm going to buy a little bulldog bitch to give me access to the international market . . .

7th circle: Castaglione

. . . patience, my angel, one day I will be yours as you will be mine, in me, and that day you will realise with icy horror that it's too late, much too late to back out or consider a withdrawal, that's right my angel, glance at your beloved sorceress, play the alpha male, get into role, head of the pack, leader of men, yet another whose mummy must have always been saying my son you are the most handsome, the cleverest, yeah right, just so you can behave in this pathetic, pathetic way, and this poor woman letting herself be tortured, a victim of her own incompetence, and she didn't exactly get a good deal from mother nature either, she must be letting herself go, it's her own fault if she won't obey the rules, poor fool, I must say her mind resembles her body, twisted and discordant, she lashed out at me during the last breakfast briefing, about the deregulation of employment rights in developing countries, internationalists of the world unite, luckily no one was listening, I bet she votes socialist, and that brute Stoeffer knocked his coffee over, I won't be inviting them next time, I'll bring de Vals and Pujol, they may be completely incompetent but at least they know how to behave in company, after all I'm the one who organises the breakfast briefings, here we go, the idiot is asking her to account for the bad debts, taking advantage to give her an ultimatum, she has two months to get them all paid, otherwise he will be forced to undertake retaliatory measures, ha, it's a battle of nerves, he wants her to resign, that kind of attitude is beyond me, humiliating someone else to establish one's own power, that's a particularly masculine perversion, men are pathetic, I'm with Valerie Solanas and the Queer Studies gang, we should neuter them all at birth, less testosterone, more peace, now there's an idea, hey, I hope Jean-Christophe hasn't been sick today, yesterday he brought up all his fish-flavoured crunchies, poor baby, it must have been to do with getting attacked at the weekend, my blood just froze when I saw that monster rushing towards him, my poor sweetheart, you fought valiantly but how could you beat an opponent ten times bigger than you, oh, I can see his master grabbing him by the collar and beating him with the leash while poor little Jean-Cri was lying on his side screaming his head off, dreadful, and then the stress of waiting at the vet's, if he hadn't survived I'd have taken out a contract on that moronic hound, an eye for an eye, a tooth for a tooth, I don't understand how Françoise can take all this without saying a word, if I was her I'd have stormed out by now, but then I'm not her, in twenty years perhaps but not yet, that idiot is frightened of me, I can tell, he must somehow sense that I'm after him, has he noticed that I'm always watching him, looking for the fatal flaw, does he realise that I know how much I turn him on, ha, if you want me you'll have to pay a heavy price, I'm a witch, I can read your soul and I know no compassion, other people's suffering amuses me, or at best leaves me cold, this meeting is pretty good in that regard, now that silly Meyer and disgusting old Tissier are under interrogation, always the same rant, no respect for internal procedures and the supervisory committee, hey, I had such a brainwave that day, poor fool Rorty was absolutely titillated, emanating great waves of desire, poor poor baby, intelligent women both arouse and terrify him, O my lion is roaring once more, as we can't seem to recover money from our clients we'll have to save it in-house, first, expense claims, recently these have been exorbitant, certain colleagues seem to think they're on some kind of luxury cruise, from now on every expense claim must be signed and validated by me personally, and as for stationery, eh Françoise, as for stationery, we'll designate a stationery officer, in addition to the work for which he is paid he will make sure that each colleague orders paper, pens and folders only when absolutely necessary, and telephones, we'll be systematically monitoring the frequency and length of calls, and demanding an explanation from any colleague who exceeds a certain threshold, and if he lies, we have the capacity to check the destination of every call, oh, my lovely alpha male, life with you is a wonderful lesson in animal behaviour, my beautiful baboon beating his chest and making shrill noises to frighten his fellow creatures, Christ taught that testosterone is the shortest route to suffering, life is a tale told by an idiot, full of sound and fury, and you can be sure that's a male idiot – because only men write history, of course, incapable of simply living their lives, men are on the outside, always outside, gesticulating, showing off, parading around, convincing themselves of how tall, strong, handsome and protective they are, when in fact they're just repeating the same pathetic scene over and over, what can you expect from such stupid, vain, slimy creatures, apart from the intense delight of watching them suffer, I like it when men adore me, when they adore me to the extent of losing themselves, losing all composure, all human dignity, poor Jean-Baptiste, you were so handsome, so affectionate, so incredibly stupid, how long did I put up with you for, three weeks, a month, I can still remember your pre-moulded speeches, you know, we the actors, the artists, the French cultural elite, the defence of the most fundamental right, the right to self-expression, what is there more vile, smug and stupid than an artist who's proud of being an artist, especially when he doesn't realise that he owes his precious remuneration to a system of solidarity whose foundations he constantly and noisily despises, at least the unemployed don't kick up such a fuss, O Rorty, my handsome alpha male, you're neither a freelance artist nor unemployed, you at least are a provider, a real provider, Rorty darling, if I seduce you then you'd better watch out, I'll take you all the way to paradise only to bring you down to earth with a bang, ha, another pseudo-indifferent glance, if he only realised all that I know about him, if he knew that each of his looks, each intonation betrays his most secret fears and deepest desires, you're as transparent and lacking in mystery as a caged rabbit, a fish in a tank, a bacteria under the blinding light of an electronic microscope, I'm looking for a man who will know how to subjugate me and I can tell it won't be you, deep down you are pathetic, as pathetic as every loser I've ever met or will meet, all men are losers, they sniff you out, follow you, shower you with compliments and presents but deep down they only care about one thing, squirting their filthy sperm deep into you, such a revolting, foul farce, O joy, Rorty is having a go at that hideous playboy Pujol, asking him to account for himself regarding the state campaign to prevent workplace accidents, how can we have lost the competition when it was almost in the bag, the final documents were approved unanimously by the client, the communications director publicly thanked the agency for the work provided and promised to call back that week after obtaining formal approval from her MD, and now there's been nothing for weeks and weeks, and we learn through the press that a competitor has won the contract, I can't understand how we can have lost more than four hundred thousand euros, winning that campaign was a fantastic financial opportunity, not to mention the consequences for our image, I am terribly shocked and disappointed, oh, look at that ass Pujol, less of a peacock today, aren't you, tiny droplets of sweat gathering on his forehead, perhaps he's worried that he won't make it through his trial period, with his lifestyle that would definitely be a problem, ha, it makes me laugh to see him like this, struggling, I've never liked his playboy arrogance, the way he ogles the young assistants, the forty-year-old man in all his splendour, the girls in my team all love him, think he's glamorous, but he reminds me of a fish, a whiting, with his round, vacant eyes, how is he going to get out of this, surely he won't start crying like that great sow Brémont, come on Pujol, make an effort, you can do it Pujol, Pu-jol, two pathetic syllables that resonate like spit on a grave, the transparency of the dead, the narcissist phase, the distinction between inner and outer, the inner flesh, the surface man, I'm handsome, mummy, look how handsome I am, the world is my mummy, I should never have slept with my psychoanalyst, let me have it all you Freudian militants, I've committed the irreparable, that's all I know how to do, commit the irreparable, I'm sick, it's incurable, I know exactly when it started, I know each and every symptom, I'm sick and I love making others sick too, love to see them crawling, like disgusting worms, how I love seeing them fatally injured, I am a Gorgon, if you look at me you'll be frozen in stone, why suffer when you can make others pay, make men pay what you yourself have suffered, for a long time all I wanted was to die, never quite managed to do it, gassing, windows, endless pills, my methods were good but I always resurfaced, memories of blinding light, multiple discordant voices, psychedelic landscapes, light-filled ghosts, marbled colours, mum's horrified face at the hospital, back to this pathetic

Pujol, he's not doing too badly, I'm disappointed, he's not stammering, not blushing, he's passing responsibility on to the Minister's principal private secretary who suddenly changed his communications team, on to the project mangers who didn't warn him in time of these changes likely to throw the confirmed agreements back into question, on to the receptionist who missed calls, in short everyone is to blame except him, handsome Pujol, what a flair for denial, what a blagger, now look at him changing the subject, all the prospects he's about to produce, his brother-in-law or something, marketing director at Vitalia, they aren't happy with their current agency, he's already been selling our service, his brother-in-law has been raving about us to the communications and HR directors, he's just waiting for the perfect moment to ram our advantage home, Rorty is still seething but Pujol is drowning him in a flood of promises, prospects and euros by the thousand, all the while committing himself to taking action against the weak links in his team, Rorty suddenly relaxes, that final argument seems to have done it, he moves on to his next victim, Tissier is waiting to hear from a fair-trade NGO, their response is imminent, the signs are good, a modest account perhaps but a wonderful opportunity for the company image, as for the Symphonium account that we talked about last time, he is getting things back on track, the dreadful management of his predecessors Sebbag and Blanchet, the way they let things go almost cost us the account, that Tissier speaks in such a scholarly, professorial tone that I almost believe him, but I suspect he's just a fantastic liar, something in his face, perhaps the contrast between his lifeless, baby elephant features and those monkey-like eyes betrays a propensity to lies and conceal-ment, blaming people who no longer work here, no, that's just too much, only to be expected really, how can he be so pathetic, and Rorty who is swallowing it all, Rorty, my little god of the gross margin, my hero of workforce reduction, you may pretend to be indifferent but I know what you're thinking and that it's all you're thinking of, I can tell, maybe one day, if you behave yourself, and straight after I'll cuckold you with Pujol, my god, what a laugh, let's hope that Jean-Christophe hasn't thrown up, perhaps there's something wrong with his stomach, perhaps that other beast pierced his spleen or his pancreas, poor little thing, he looks so cute asleep on the sofa, with his itty-bitty tongue hanging out of his impish little face, it makes me want to kiss him, to cuddle him like a gor-geous little love child, let's hope his injuries don't produce any after-effects, I should get some ultrasound whistles, they're the only way to fend off these crazed dogs, then I wouldn't have to witness such outbursts of brute violence, alpha males are so bloodthirsty, always gagging for a fight, but I know how to make them as gentle as lambs, just a few ounces lighter and the world becomes a much better, much kinder place, just a few little ounces, now there's an idea, Rorty is continuing round the table, questioning Roussel about the restructuring of the creative department, Roussel replies that the restructuring has started, the old teams are on their way out, and new teams have been simultaneously taken on, the computer stock refurbished, the storage capacity improved, the archiving and digitising of all files has been facilitated, as recently as last Friday an IT meeting took place, the staff were told about the new company rules and invited to negotiate their departure if they weren't willing to respect them, there have already been two resignations and one settlement amongst the sound team, soon only Benoit will be left, he costs us two thousand five hundred euros and gets through a tremendous amount of work, at that price we can keep him, at least that gives us one permanent member of staff to do the routine work, Rorty agrees, that Roussel is so boring, only just started and he's already so drab, and then he acts so aloof, so ironic, I don't belong here, I'm just passing through but I've found you all very amusing, I hate cynics more than anything, so horribly pathetic, they pretend to be proud of an attitude that they didn't choose because deep down they refuse to take responsibility, like ugly people who make themselves even more ugly to demonstrate how little they care about their physical appearance, and that block-head Alighieri, what is he staring at with such intensity, the sky perhaps, hang on, I must be dreaming, Rorty is grilling him and he hardly deigns to reply, just keeps staring at who knows what, my god, he's so weird, must be completely out of it, unless he's asleep with his eyes open, funny boy that Alighieri, well educated, Catholic school, ex-art critic, as enigmatic as he is pleased with himself, Rorty is back on to Tissier, who replies with his usual haughtiness, the guy is hideous, I feel sorry for his wife, he's in the middle of a divorce apparently, he deserves it, I hope she gets good alimony, I should start thinking about it myself, getting married, starting a family, it's about time, although I would need to find a man, but no, stupid me, I've found the man, just need to wait for the right moment for our life together to take root, after Tissier it will be my turn, thirty seconds to think of a theme for my next breakfast briefing . . .

8th circle: Rorty

. . . 12.44, one item left, then lunch with Fischer, he'll be grilling me on the budget forecast again, my belly hurts already, bloody guts, always giving out at just the wrong moment, quick, distract myself so I don't have to rush to the loo, SHE is describing the theme of her forthcoming series of breakfast briefings, ethical marketing, yes, that's an excellent, excellent concept, slight toss of the head, haughty bearing, magnificent forehead, intoxicating mouth, bewitching voice, if SHE only knew how much I want her, SHE has nothing but excellent, excellent ideas, I too have nothing but excellent, excellent ideas, we are made for each other, I wowed them with Nietzsche again, those online philosophy crammers are excellent, I'll have to read the whole thing one day, if I ever have time, so many words, and books and concepts to digest, best to head straight for the main point, among the emerging trends in marketing, consumers taking working conditions into account, soft, husky voice, elegant neck, eyes like coals, don't look at her, pretend to ignore her, act unimpressed, cynical, SHE mustn't suspect for a moment that I want her, then lunch with Fischer, I already know the gist, blackmail, threats, etc, if you don't win two big new accounts by the end of the year we'll have to review the terms of our collaboration, we have set targets for you, and you only have one quarter left in which to achieve or better still exceed them, there's a long way to go, better move up a gear, ouch, my guts, then I'll play the good old cutback card, the supreme weapon, the top trump of the desperate director, lightening the wage bill, dumping ballast to compensate for the depressed economic climate and get back to a strong operating margin, oh, nothing too drastic, thirty per cent of the workforce by the end of the year, at a rate of eight or nine dismissals per month over six months so as to bypass the legislation, no one will be any the wiser, ah, now that's a good idea, that'll relax my poor old guts, chill man, everything's cool, I'm the cleaner with manicured hands, the exterminating angel with spotless wings, the blue-eyed serial killer, right, who shall I start with among this lot, Meyer, no, she's been here too long, her clients are loyal, losing them would be the last straw, Pujol, that idiot Pujol, now there's a good idea, still in his trial period, considering what he brings in, no mercy for Pujol, dodgy night-owl Pujol, Brémont too, dreadful body, lets herself go, no confidence, come on, be off with you, and Tissier, our dear Tissier, so pretentious, so boring, so unattractive, but I'd be a fool to let him go, I feel so handsome and strong and clever in comparison, as for the other alcoholic, that Stoeffer is another kettle of fish, still staring at me so weirdly, how dare he squint at me like that, he hates me, at least with him it's obvious, no mistaking it, I should have fired him ages ago but something has always held me back, fear perhaps, yes, fear, he's a brutish lout that Stoeffer, capable of anything, of dreadful things, de Vals gets on my nerves but he does bring in the cash, expert strategist, superbly aggressive salesman, a great instrument of warfare, proof that there are high-performing, competitive, *normal* staff out there, apart from HER of course, but then SHE is something else entirely, better than an employee, my potential future mistress, no, my future mistress pure and simple, I need to attack on all fronts, take her by surprise if possible, nothing better than a well-managed blitzkrieg for conquering a new continent, watch out, Columbus, Cortés and Drake, next week there's the big corporate communications prize ceremony, a bit of bubbly then drive HER back home, right, enough of this digression, I need to focus and continue with this wretched go-round, on to Clément-Dourville, what an old hag, misery guts, gives the company such a bad image, surely I can make her resign, got to move up a gear, Roussel, don't know yet, wait till he's finished the first part of his trial period, we can always renew it, as for that blockhead Alighieri, if he knew his days in the company were numbered perhaps he'd stop being such a waster and taking the piss out of me like this, not remotely with the programme that Alighieri, and so arrogant, he contradicted me in public the other day, who does he think he is, moron, bloody intellectual git, just because he has a philosophy doctorate and is published in god knows what obscure avant-garde literary journal, I do write books myself you know, pathetic loser, sub-shithead, I'm going to squash you like an insect, I'll have you out of here in a fortnight with the help of preliminary discussions and recorded delivery letters, bloody workforce, it's because of you that Fischer will be hassling me again, aha, green capital, respect for the environment, corporate social responsibility, brands committing themselves to making the world a fairer, more beautiful, more liveable place, essential elements in consumer attractiveness, if SHE only knew how little I care about any of that but how much I want her, HER, I can just see her, naked, lustful and cruel, I melt into that beautiful, perfect image, Jean-François Rorty, company director, married, two children, a new mistress, so what, as long as no one loses face, Audrey won't know, what could be more natural than cheating on your wife when you're an overworked, overstressed company director, I can see her now, my poor dear husband, all those late-night meetings and having to work at the weekends, lying comes naturally to men, only animals and losers never lie, Audrey, my beautiful Audrey de Ribancourt, our wedding was a magnificent success but our relationship is going to the dogs, Audrey, beautiful Audrey, you are so beautiful, so perfect, so absolutely proper that I have never loved you, a show-couple, an alibi-couple, with a life as beautiful as an ad in an international style magazine, Audrey, beautiful Audrey, you don't love me either, you have never loved me and I don't give a damn, if you think I don't know what you're up to with your four grand a week courses in the laying on of hands, I can see it now, al fresco orgies, ritual debauchery, bacchanalian frolics in the moonlight, all organised by one of the thousands of hippy gurus in the Ardeche, the silly goose has a lover, I'm sure of it, she's cheating on me with a hippy guru, that would explain her most recent quirks, the way she talks in riddles, her gaze both distant and languorous, her sudden passion for yoga and tarot cards, her seaweed and tofu diet, but how exquisite THIS woman is, if she only knew how much I want her, de Vals has interrupted, he agrees wholeheartedly with Sophie and would like to just touch on a related issue, brand psycho-analysis, not a bad looking kid that de Vals, strong face, tanned complexion showing off intense black eyes, athletic build, a young alpha male, brand psychoanalysis, yes, good idea, perhaps the only useful outcome of that stupid invention, libido, repression, castration complex, narcissist stage, what quackery, hey, *Living, Thinking and Feeling Better without Freud*, that was a good book, glory to the cognitive sciences, glory to empirical certitude, the human being is nothing more than a simple collection of atoms, molecules and electrochemical currents, some function better than others, end of story, what need for mystery, after my book comes out I'd better work on this, bring out another one with some brilliant title like *The Ultimate Mystery* or *The Far Reaches of Mystery*, with the mystery being that in fact there is no mystery, backed up by cognitive science and behavioural therapies, a kind of anti-psychoanalysis manual, in which I'll also tackle mystical and esoteric idiocies through the ages, druidism, shamanism, taoism, sufism, animism, I can see the cover now, I'll be on all the TV shows, that'll really seduce her, SHE will be absolutely crazy about me, SHE is so beautiful, so exotic, the only problem is her bloody hound, I'd have to put up with him too, oh, so easy to fall out of a sixth-floor window, no, just kidding, as long as SHE doesn't sleep with it, bloody allergies, all that invisible molecular activity really turns my stomach, oh yes, must tell Audrey to get the cleaning lady in twice a day, there was fluff under the living room sofa, that filthy dust really puts the wind up me, especially since reading that article on the contaminants found in the blood of several British MPs, or were they European, can't remember exactly, you can die from that stuff, and from animals, to think that I've never been to the tropics, scared of getting bitten by all those fucking insects, last month I couldn't visit Bart in his Yucatan villa because of a panic attack, had to turn back at the airport on the pretext of sciatica, waking nightmares of snakes and spiders crawling into my mouth, my nose, my ears, cold sweats, guts on fire, panicking that I'd be swallowing deadly bacteria as soon as I stepped out of the plane, as long as no one ever finds out, I can already see the mocking smiles of the staff, the competition, the international market, the share-holders, the murderous professional press, The Truth Revealed on the Phobias of Jean-François Rorty, Chief Executive of KLS, he's never been to the tropics because he's scared stiff of snakes and spiders, that's it, now I'm thinking about Fischer again, this is dreadful, his eyes make me so nervous, his implacable authority paralyses me, how I'd love to fulfil each of his demands but he sets the bar too high, much too high, my god, how can he be so strong and me so weak, the more intransigent and threatening he is the more I fall apart, scattered in a thousand pieces and rendered hope-less by pains and suicidal thoughts, but when he compliments me I float above the ground, wildly grateful, finding him enormously handsome, almost wanting to throw myself at him and kiss him, sublimely confused, as stupidly happy as a schoolgirl given a gold star by her teacher, SHE will soon have finished her presentation and in a few minutes it will be back to me, Stoeffer is stroking his moustache and badly trimmed beard and frowning, the guy revolts me, he's brimming over with dirty hate, Alighieri is doing his transcendental meditation thing, he'll be levitating in a minute, no worries Alighieri, I'll help you back down, Pujol is looking at his shoes, Tissier – still just as gormless – is picking his nose, Brémont is watching Tissier pick his nose, bloody workforce, what a pathetic sight, and SHE among them, and Fischer waiting to trip me up, oh, his demanding eyes and implacable wrinkles as he asks me for this month's accounts, the only way out is to grovel, to sink lower, ever lower, losing all human dignity, becoming as lowly as an earthworm, a larva, a cockroach, floundering in a bog of stock-market waste, eating variably-priced excrement, SHE will soon have finished her great speech, I'll soon be seeing Fischer, let's hope SHE hasn't decided to eat at the same restaurant, she mustn't see me with him, or even worse, what if Fischer invites her to lunch, too, Fischer might seduce her, my worst nightmare, stop, don't think about Fischer, I need some detachment here, I'm trapped, nowhere to go, like a rat, trapped between the beauty of this woman with her infinite gaze and the nightmare of Fischer, help, my old friend, come to my rescue and tell me that none of this matters, that it will all be OK in the end, oh my inescapable future, my constant companion, that's it, I can feel your icy white caress, death is a lack of good manners, Pierre Dac, I'm glad you're here, you're the only one who understands, the only one who knows the true value of things, vanity of vanities, all is vanity, Ecclesiastes, this time it's happening, I am dead, to me the kingdom of darkness, dark corridors ending in light, calls in the dark, a bombardment of feelings, the porous solitude of endless space, help, I can't see, all I can see is the nightmare of Fischer, my bowels, again and always these bloody bowels, this fucking body, a mass of decomposing flesh, rot among the swine, I'll have to dash to the loo, these bloody organs, shit machines, repositories of filth and germs, hurrah for the future, hurrah for disease prevention, prosthetics and intelligent matter, hey, there's an idea for a book, *A Brilliant Farewell to the Body*, I could write the *Farewell to the Body*, shit, it's already been written by some anthropologist, can't remember his name, oh well, I can still praise the splendour of future worlds and become the

Huxley of the noughties, a *Brave New World* is within our grasp, I shall describe it, great visionary that I am, SHE is looking at me, SHE has nearly finished her presentation, SHE is all I want from life, or death, or anything, don't forget to bring up the roof terrace, and then lunch with Fischer, no, I'm not a visionary, just a ratty company director with bad guts, oh that Alighieri, still away with the fairies, I hate him, I don't know why I hate him so much but if it was only down to me I'd get rid of him immediately, and Audrey who keeps inviting her new friends from the Ardeche round, what a shabby-looking bunch, actors, artists, ethnologists, educators, playwrights, writers, with their pseudo-cool attitudes, I'm so at ease in my astral body, in my cosmic life, they were there again last night, sprawling on my ten-grand sofas, I felt their contempt immediately, their hatred for the successful businessman, the patron, fucking artists, vile mob of left-wing pseudo-intellectuals, social workers and politically correct community fuckwits, who do they think they are, losers, cash is the only tangible value, the only objective variable you can trade on any market, even the art market, what irony, proves that their world is far from an enchanted cocoon immune to the laws of supply and demand, I hate artists, odd-jobbing poodles, creators of hot air, the last contemporary art fair was pathetic, shameful, all that rubbish set up as masterpieces, there's no more beauty in that load of crap than in a dustbin or a bog roll, hey, now there's a good idea, I'll exhibit a dustbin and call it a work of art, SHE is so entrancing, Fischer in five minutes, the budget, my guts, bloody workforce, bloody market, oh to be an artist, rich, famous and adored, not a stressed-out company director . . .

9th circle: Clément-Dourville

. . . unidentifiable icy current between navel and solar plexus, a tempest of filth, no longer say a word, collapse, the ambulance, the road, the trees, the catheters, like Hubert, eternal rest, close my eyes and no longer see a thing, nothing but the vile face of the filth gnawing at my solar plexus, the waves, always these icy waves, the static yet swirling horror moving, why must the world be so hard, why so cold, disappear, disappear, fall into an endless sleep and turn into something else, a dog, a tree or a wall of granite, anything but this body in which I always feel as if I'm falling, icy waves flooding my solar plexus, lifeless eyes staring at me, I must get a grip on myself, my life, what life, Daddy has lost his mind, the other day he thought I was Jean-Claude, so sad, he was always our bedrock, our guide, and Hubert will be gone soon, Delphine doesn't want to see us anymore, Rorty is attacking me and I can't think what else to respond, old lady, I'm such an old lady all of a sudden, sickly and hideous, I've lost even more weight, my teeth are coming loose, my wrinkles are deepening, there's no more humanity in the eyes of these profit-crazed men than in the cogs of a lift, the world of work, my only distraction, my final refuge, no longer safe, besieged by the diktat of short-term financial imperatives, the tiny corner of reality I've spent years building is starting to crack, nothing will stop its destruction, I've given everything to my work but it no longer wants me, I'll be stuck alone with myself, with Hubert's death, with Daddy's decline and my own solitude, still that icy wind inside me, the ground giving way, and these ghostly, mutating, inhuman faces, my sedatives are powerless to ward off this ever-encroaching horror, day and night, without respite, last night I had that nightmare again, always the same one, that horrible house, Hubert is there, and some of the staff too, immobile, blurry, I speak to them but no one replies, and suddenly I know, I know they are dead, I know that this house is a house of the dead and that nothing is left, not joy, not dreams, not hope . . . apart from these nightmares I can't sleep at all, my nights are hideous and the days even worse, these men are alive but their eyes are dead, as dead as those ghosts haunted by the sudden emptiness of leaving their bodies, collapse, the ambulance, the road, the trees, the catheters, like Hubert, eternal rest, close my eyes and no longer see a thing, nothing but the waves, always these icy waves, Hubert will soon be gone, he's been hospitalised for a fourth time, his heart failed again after a triple bypass, the doctors' prognosis was clear, and Delphine, she hasn't even phoned to ask after her father, what exactly does she resent us for, I've never understood it, never known what the hell was going on in her mind, what does she say about us to her fiancé, or her friends, what awfulness has she gone and invented to justify her silence, my god, how did we give birth to such a cold, indifferent, rancorous creature, how did we let her grow so distant, and the family, what family, Hubert will soon be gone, close my eyes and see nothing, nothing but the vile face of the filth gnawing at my solar plexus, the waves, always these icy waves, the static yet swirling horror moving, petrifaction of the flesh, the mind and everything else, the knowledge that everything is at rock bottom but could get worse, that the worst is yet to come, that each second contains the promise of even greater suffering, that much as I've been torn apart, crushed, wrecked, overwhelmed by this horror, the fact of it will be harder still, fight, fight so as not to drown, look at the sky, the lovely sky, wonderful white clouds, the calm sight of them drifting, Alighieri is watching the sky, Alighieri is contemplating the superb white clouds, Alighieri, perhaps the only living being in this whole meeting, can he restore my hope, hope, what an absurd word, so far away, try despite everything to cling to it, to cling to him as to a lifeline, contemplate the sky as he does, curl up in his happiness, his happiness, a glimmer, an illusion, papier mâché scenery, illusion giving way to illusion, the lifeline snaps, we don't live under the same sky, this light is too much for me, the blue too bright, Hubert will soon be gone, I will leave this company that I have spent so many years developing, an image of lice crushed next to a cigarette butt, it's raining ash, the butt has disappeared, everything has been burnt, nothing can stop me losing myself, plunging once and for all into the eternal silence of this icy smoke, eternal rest, close my eyes and no longer see a thing, the waves, the deadly waves, ice prison, static decomposition, slow putrefaction, why this world, why this cold, disappear, go away, far away, sleep, an endless sleep and transformation into something else, anything, table, pen, electric socket, air-conditioning filter, coffee machine, electromagnetic ray, tree, outside they are sending out their first leaves, the trees, outside, so reassuring and yet so unreal, lose myself in them, leave this body in which I always feel as if I'm falling, rabbit, I see a little rabbit, he's sick, he's crying, poor little rabbit, poor little human, a corpse-in-waiting worn down by his inevitable destiny, they are here, all around, everywhere, calling to us from their swarming, cellular world, Hubert will soon be gone, help, help me, quick, a rope, my work is my rope, a rope that is sinking, being swallowed up, move offices, meeting, Rorty, vile Rorty, as vile as the dead in my nightmares, that inorganic, grey world in which all hope is banished, I live in exile and can see no possible way out, what to do, where to go when death seems the same as life, when you're too tired, too weary to prefer one thing to anything else, human beings, love of life, an old-fashioned equation, I loved Hubert, I loved Daddy, I loved my job, this move is yet another form of torture, he's going in for the kill, if I were a believer I might see it as an opportunity, a challenge from the Almighty to help me attain a state of grace, to find the beyond in which I have never believed, I am desperately atheist and profoundly desperate, life expectancy is increasing by more than three months every year, that's an irrefutable fact, despite the pollution of the ground water, climate chaos, increased rates of cancer and the unavoidable rise in work-related illnesses, life expectancy is going up by more than three months every year, the smiling faces of the scientists interviewed on the TV, the smiling face of the newscaster, the horror of those bared teeth, suddenly none of it makes sense, he is happy, smiling, suddenly none of the physiological or molecular or whatever background makes any sense, none of what makes this situation possible, Hubert will soon be gone, my father has lost his mind and I will soon be chucked out like an old dishrag, perfect me, hardworking me, who has always given this company my all, and has never begrudged my time or energy to defend the company's best interests, Rorty's plan is so obvious, he wants to make the legal department a crèche for young wolves working fourteen-hour days, he is going to dismiss all my staff, use me for the restructuring then chuck me out and take on a cost-killer, a proper cost-killer, my humanist management style makes him laugh, that man despises me, that man is looking at me as a snake looks at a rabbit, hey little rabbit, he's watching me again, the threatening gaze of a bloodthirsty brute, still trotting out some bloody management theory, he looks delighted with himself, his eyes are sparkling, there's a hint of a smile on his soulless lips, he's quoting Nietzsche again, Hitler's favourite philosopher, rediscover your predatory instinct dulled by centuries of Judeo-Christian morality, conquer every market, be prepared to bring your opponent to his knees, being good isn't good enough, you've got to be the best, and if you're not up for this adventure then tough luck, natural selection will take care of it, let's be eagles, not lambs, the company, cemetery of dreams, grey polyurethane box where the sad thoughts of overworked managers die their death, carpets jarred by the uncertain steps of targets not met, transparent corridors, open spaces mirroring destroyed souls, torn to pieces by the extreme pressure of short-term financial imperatives, stress, blackmail, moral abuse, blood pressure problems, musculoskeletal issues, total or partial disability with one hundred per cent incapacity benefit, subcontracting to developing countries where children have to work and prostitute themselves, I can't understand this, when I've always made sure that each member of staff is treated with respect and consideration, I no longer understand, I understand nothing because I am nothing, nothing more than a bag of pain, the horror is everywhere and peace nowhere, an image of baby koalas irradiated under a green sky, the end of the animal reign, the dying throes of the plant world, humanity has never existed, only mineral life survives, nothing can stop me losing myself, plunging for ever into the eternal silence of a block of granite, more flashbacks to my nightmare, that horrible house, Hubert, the staff, Rorty in the middle with Richard Stoeffer and Sophie Castaglione watching him, they are all facing me, I'm speaking to them and they're ignoring me and suddenly I know, I know they are dead, I know that this house is a house of the dead and that there is nothing left, not joy, not dreams, not hope, apart from these nightmares I can't sleep at all, the forces of death are nibbling at life, my life without him, my life without them, my life without life, unidentifiable icy current between navel and solar plexus, a tempest of detritus in the silence, no longer say a word, collapse, the ambulance, the road, the trees, the catheters, like Hubert, eternal rest, I live in my dream, little doll's house at the edge of the galaxy, home to the living dead, the eternally sick, so tortured and pained that they cannot die, close my eyes and no longer see a thing, nothing but the vile face of the filth creeping over every possible horizon, the waves, again and always these icy waves, the static yet swirling horror moving, the rotting of the flesh and the mind, the knowledge that everything is at rock bottom but could become worse, that the worst is still to come, that each second contains the promise of even greater suffering, that much as I've been torn apart, crushed, wrecked, overwhelmed by this horror, the fact of it will be harder still, life, a moment's horror in the midst of a void, like that dream of formless, lifeless bustling, a morbid mineral whirl, I am not dead but I'm no longer among the living, the shimmering, hope-swollen universe of these men with their conquering eyes is foreign to me, so foreign, to conquer, always to conquer, contemptible colonists, the eradication of pre-Columbus America, the genocidal massacre of the American Indians, the Armenians, the slave trade, ethnic cleansing in Serbia and Rwanda, myriad torture and death camps, vision of a concentration camp in the early hours, the fog clearing to reveal that THAT happened, the years and the centuries may pass but no one and nothing will be able to erase that, I remember my mother on her deathbed, exhausted, disfigured by pain and by morphine, she was always lecturing me about eternal peace and the eternal life of the blessed but she experienced nothing except the sheer horror of illness, history is faltering, humanity is suffocating itself and Hubert will soon be gone, rabbit, little dying rabbit, I see nothing but you, rabbit, little bloodied rabbit, you are my friend, I'm entering a place of threat and darkness in which I can see nothing, nothing but miserable shadows tossing restlessly, happiness, liberation, grace, redemption, holiness, all placebo words, affirmations for the masses, the smallness of genius, of the great humanist ideals, of the democratic dream, of education, scientific progress and all the systems of social protection, faced with the immensity of the void, Rorty, still Rorty, Rorty is a mountain peak, a peninsula, a monument to the glory of conquest, Rorty, tiny on the inside yet sneering, Rorty and the thirst for power, Rorty and progress, Rorty and opportunities for development, Rorty and his endless breakthroughs, Rorty is looking at me and smiling, the little house smile, I can see into his fetid thoughts, little house with smiling ceilings, smiling floorboards, smiling walls, and that girl Castaglione, she's smiling too, the horror of all these bared, mechanical teeth, nightmare, nightmare, nightmare, nightmare, nightmare, nightmare, nightmare, nightmare, nightmare, nightmare, nightmare, nightmare, nightmare, nightmare, the teeth remind me of that horrible house, Hubert, the staff, Arnaud de Vals, Richard Stoeffer, Sophie Castaglione, Anne-Laure Brémont, Pierre-Henry Tissier and the others, the absolute realness of that little house of the dead, everything else is just illusion, close my eyes and no longer see a thing, nothing but the vile face of the filth gnawing at my solar plexus, the waves, always these icy waves, extreme speed of the horror turning to perfect stillness, past, present, future, all united in the knowledge that everything is at rock bottom but could become worse, that the worst is still to come, that each second contains the promise of even greater suffering, that much as I've been torn apart, crushed, wrecked, overwhelmed by this horror, the fact of it will be harder still, Mummy is in one corner of the little house, holding the rabbit, the little white rabbit, one of his eyes has been gouged out, he's losing a lot of blood, he's struggling with all his rabbit might but my mother is holding him by his paws and sniggering, a knife sparkling in her left hand, actually it isn't Mummy, she looks just like her but it's not really her, same hairstyle, same eyes, same body but something about her terrifies me, something unspeakable and invisible tells me to flee this evil woman, I try to leave but at the same time realise that my feet won't obey, will no longer obey, fear is paralysing me, I'm condemned to remain still, like a statue, petrified, the woman keeps coming closer, collapse, the ambulance, the road, the trees, the catheters, like Hubert, eternal rest, close my eyes and no longer see a thing, except the waves, always the waves, nothing but the waves, return to childhood, happy childhood with Mummy and Daddy in the 2CV, holidays, delight on the La Rochelle coastline as the great stretch of blue reveals itself in shimmering glimpses as we drove, from an embankment or the crest of a hill, excitement at the first whiff of salt water, and then the ocean, the immense ocean coming ever closer . . .

Purgatory

Roussel

. . . what the fuck am I doing here, surrounded by these card-carrying lunatics, why have they included me in their strategy committee, I haven't even completed my trial period, so much the better, I can leave without giving notice, perhaps I should, I knew that the corporate world was tough but not this tough, when I see this great pile-up of frustration, pain, resentment and Ubuesque lust for power it makes me want to curl up like a baby, leave never to return, I came here to manage teams, not to lay-off people I don't even know, and yet the only thing they're interested in is reducing the wage bill, shaving expenses, that's all they can talk about, their eyes are riveted to the blue line of the operating margin, this Rorty is grotesque, his eulogy to evolution is a farce, the company as site of institutionalised predation, now there's a good thesis subject, to side with the dominant or the dominated, your choice comrade, all men are born and remain free and equal in law, except here, in the profit factory, trample others to stage a takeover, merge with and acquire their energy, declare their psychological and physiological integrity bankrupt, all in total legality, this Rorty is such a caricature, and all these morons hanging on his every word,

well, not all of them, some of them look horrified, that poor
Françoise Clément-Dourville is deathly pale, she reminds me
of that friend of mum's, such a sad little lady, who lived alone
in a castle and ended up killing herself, Mrs Gassendi, yes,
Mrs Gassendi, the same receding chin, the same huge forehead, the same round eyes sunken into sockets encircled by
dark shadows, I must be a masochist to keep staring at her
when she freaks me out so much, she clearly hasn't even
noticed, I must be totally invisible to her, oh well, make the
most of the opportunity to discreetly check out the others,
that de Vals for instance, interesting case, the morphological
and physiognomic indications are clear, the man is a dick,
literally, yes, or a ferret, with his little bald dolichocephalic
warrior's head just aching to charge whoever he's speaking to,
rustic skull, plant-like neck, oh, if he knew how little I think of
him, and he looks so proud, arrogance personified, I really
don't like that guy, if I was Rorty I'd be watching him like a
hawk, but let them destroy each other, it's all so typical, so
pathetic, Pujol, trapped in his posture of attractive, young,
dynamic, motivated manager, poor guy, he's such a cliché
it hurts, hey, I'm a hero, not only bright but handsome too,
I've been to the best universities, I've got a big motor and
huge responsibilities, or vice versa, what did he study in fact,
business I think, yeah, business and an MBA in some trendy,
annoying new HR trend, oops, he just noticed me watching
him, must have seen me frowning, quick, look elsewhere,
subtly, act as if I haven't noticed that he saw me, focus on

Tissier instead, the incredible Tissier, busy picking his nose in the middle of a meeting, oblivious, as if there were a thick screen between him and the rest of the world, or as if, thanks to a fairy godmother or a benevolent company fairy he had become invisible, benevolent company fairy, now there's a contradiction in terms, Dominique Meyer is looking at him reproachfully, he really is disgusting, manners, Tissier, manners, first lesson, don't pick your nose, fart, vomit or wipe your bum during a meeting, second lesson, do everything you can to be as attractive as possible, that's it, I'm sickened, I feel like throwing up, that Tissier revolts me, I can just imagine his scuzzy private parts and grubby underwear, come on, focus on Meyer, pretty little thing, looks a bit down in the dumps, she really does, why, quick, intuitive diagnosis, close my eyes, focus on her presence, I can see her, she's going back to her apartment, a cute little building in the fifteenth arrondissement with a balcony, a door code and off-street parking, it's already dark, she switches on the hall light, dumps her things on the living-room sofa, listens to the answer phone, glances at the paintings on the wall as she does every evening, a feeling of emptiness, as every evening, her husband isn't home yet, he's a chief executive, investment banker, financial director or international lawyer, some kind of important job, he'll only be home in two hours, maybe four, or perhaps he's still away on secondment, she is looking after their little girl by herself, oh yes, I forgot, first she went to collect the child from the nanny's, thinking to herself that she doesn't get much help from her flighty husband, he doesn't listen to her, barely looks at her and no longer touches her, perhaps he has a mistress, or who knows, a male lover, she should discuss it with her girlfriends but they are all so busy too, in conclusion, she'd do well to seek satisfaction with a young, energetic guy with a good sense of humour, hey, calm it my friend, you're as good as married, four years' cohabitation isn't to be sniffed at, not to be sniffed at for sure, but then neither are Dominique Meyer's curves to be sniffed at, especially compared to the other two, between that bovine Brémont and Castaglione the praying mantis, no question, at least Meyer seems sane, soft, sensual, a little neurotic perhaps but just right, really, normal, I'd bet my bottom dollar that Castaglione is a man-eater, one of those crazy bitches who spends her life trying to demonstrate that you're the most pathetic loser, and generally succeeding, their technique is to start from the self-fulfilling prophecy that I am the all-powerful and you are the total loser, and that if I'm with you, you'd better watch out – whoever you are and whatever you do, every one of your actions will prove my thesis, a perverse system, not only does the observer influence the results but is an integral part of them, but to get back to my point, one thing is for sure I don't want to become as embittered as this lot, this is my second firm and it's exactly the same story, pain and resentment at every level, there's still time to turn back, branch off, OK, fine, branch off, but towards what, I could finish my dissertation, yeah, why not, finish my dissertation – or start it at least – and then a doctorate, easy, I've got my subject, the company as site of institutionalised predation, the world of work from the perspective of the findings of Garfinkel, the ethnomethodology of the office, in a manner of speaking, now there's a fine idea, and then I'll teach, except that to teach you have to become a professor, or at least a fellow, three hundred candidates for every job, not exactly a done deal, not a done deal perhaps but not impossible, better than this anyway, better than being the cog linking client-mad sales people and stressed-out graphic designers, yes, teaching, could be the perfect solution for escaping this noxious hospice-type environment, well, not the perfect solution perhaps, working for myself would be the perfect solution, Roussel & Co, communication consultants, yes, why not, but then it's goodbye to weekends, holidays, lounging around in bed with my little Marie, no, that's out, my relationship is sacred, perhaps I should follow Patrick's advice, take the civil service exams, yes, why not, the civil service exams, I could become a top civil servant, now there's a way to make a decent living, remain independent and have reasonable status, without sacrificing holidays and weekends, I could disagree with my boss without being sacked, when I spoke just now Rorty was staring at me, searching out my weak point, that jerk is constantly and systematically looking to destabilise others in order to assert his own power, the simple dichotomy of corporate human relations, dominate or be dominated, and dominate by any means possible, so watch out, beware, if you disagree with the boss you're liable to be out on your ear, just because Rorty hired me doesn't mean I owe him absolute loyalty and trust, yes, the civil service exams are a great idea, I'm going to study for them, I'll start swotting tonight, law and history, actually, tonight is Peggy's birthday, impossible, tomorrow then, oh no, I've promised to play squash with David tomorrow, the day after then, yes, starting the day after tomorrow I'll study for the civil service exams, perhaps I should call Jean-Charles, he's got a friend who passed them and found a good job in the Treasury, yes, ask him for a few tips on studying for the exams, I'm not going to simply rot away here but you do have to be realistic, just because I'm going to study for the civil service exams doesn't mean that everything's going to stop as if by magic, quite the opposite, in the meantime I've got to work hard, get a permanent position, once the trial period is over I can at least freewheel a bit, I can't give up all this for some fanciful dream, can't give up my only source of income for a hypothetical admission to France's most prestigious university, and Marie is so anxious, so afraid of going without, money issues really freak her out, our relationship is still fragile, I'm not exactly going to risk everything on a childish whim, I'm not twenty-one any more, if I resign I'll get nothing, how would I manage the rent, twelve hundred euros a month, what would we live on, her freelance fees and artist subsidies wouldn't exactly cover it, while she's making a name for herself I've no choice, jobs don't grow on trees, especially not jobs paid over six thousand euros a month, in spite of everything I am lucky to be here, well, luck is a relative thing, I need to keep reminding myself that the only point of this place is where it might lead, into senior government perhaps, or politics, yes, why not politics, Frank is always suggesting that I attend his council meetings, that's an exciting prospect, there's no way I'm going to linger here for ever, full of resentment and contempt, no way I'm going to live in fear of dismissal like a cockroach at the mercy of some bloody boot, this firm must be no more than a phase, a moment leading to another moment, being trapped here until retirement would be hell, becoming the old guy, the incompetent, the wash-out the younger guys keep shoving onto the hard shoulder, like that poor Clément-Dourville, the woman seems so unhappy, why is it so hard to look away from her lined face, her misery, she really gets me down but it's stronger than me, I can't help looking at her, a bit like worrying a sore tooth, what is her life like, her family, does she even have a family, what does she do in her spare time, I tell you what, I'd rather put a bullet in my brain than become like her, as sad and wretched as her, now I'm upset, the woman emanates something so terrible, so distressing, what secret agony, what tragedy is going on inside her, I don't know and I don't want to know, Alighieri, opposite me, high as a kite, hey, I'd never noticed he was such a lunatic, strange guy, don't think he's flavour of the month at the moment, the naughty boy can't have won enough accounts, but at least he still looks fresh, not too corrupted by the system, and that Rorty is still droning on, he's exhausting,

I'm not listening, I don't want to listen to him any more, a man electrified by the furious desire to dominate other men, constantly repeating and re-scripting his wretched fantasies of omnipotence, to other men who have only one wish, to be in his place, that's how this system keeps going, when will he collapse, will he ever collapse, Rorty is asking me a question, no, false alarm, he's just looking at me, his gaze shining with fervour, that polka-dot tie is pretty tasteless, Nietzsche, always Nietzsche, just the guy to turn the young predators on to his philosopho-managerial twaddle, personally I prefer Schopenhauer, or even Bergson, the will to live, vital force, the creative power of consciousness, all much more pertinent than this notion of the will to power so overused in the marketplace, and what about compassion, a cardinal virtue for Schopenhauer and Bergson not to mention Buddhism, the cardinal virtue of all human relations, yet not found in Nietzsche, or only as a negative, Nietzsche, still Nietzsche, always Nietzsche, why doesn't he quote Foucault, Deleuze, Habermas or Sloterdijk, because he doesn't know them, Jesus, he's never read them, I'd bet my bottom dollar, this Rorty is pig ignorant, knows nothing of philosophy, of the world of thought, that's why he keeps reducing it to such primary-school orthodoxy, I should tell him loud and clear, stand on the table, cup my hands around my mouth and yell that idiocy can take many forms, including that of pleasant Nietzschean banter, I can just see Rorty's face, and the others, what would happen, perhaps nothing, perhaps they'd all pretend they hadn't heard, and Rorty would carry on with his tirade regardless, the company, site of contemporary confusion, at heart we're all here because we didn't actively choose, because our will-to-power faltered when it came into contact with reality, because we didn't dream hard enough to become pro footballers, movie stars, successful authors or even to just follow our own path, as a child I wanted to be a clown, to play the fool in front of a crowd, the thought of it made me so happy, so crazily hopeful, it was my destiny, my vocation, why did I stray from that path, was it really my path, is there a pre-existent path or does the path get built as we tread it, a huge question, the only thing I know is that I'd better leave this one before too long, what if I took Rorty to court for sexual harassment like in *American Beauty,* I might win a fortune in compensation, I can see Rorty's face now, actually I don't want to do the civil service exams, I want to go to circus school, why not, after all I wouldn't be the first person to start again from scratch, I've no children, no insurmountable constraints, yes, it's got to be possible, as long of course as I'm determined enough, no good sitting cosily at home watching life go by, a DVD here, a gig there, a dinner here, a bit of squash there, mustn't let life go gently by without me, without my even noticing, mustn't get all bourgeois and end up in a cul-de-sac, come on, buck up my friend, create your own destiny, you just need Rorty-level determination, I'll manage, focus all my energy in one direction, will, passion, self-government, mustn't waste my life, this clown idea makes me happy, there lies salvation, it's up to me, I'm a free man, life is long and the future belongs to me . . .

Paradise

Alighieri

. . . what joy to be here, alive, among my fellow men, the sky is so beautiful and I feel so light today, as light as a breeze wafting through the Acropolis on a summer's eve, as luminous as a ray of winter sun on the Sorbonne, I nearly died last night and yet I'm here, alive, in the world, among these men who are, despite everything, my fellow creatures, my brothers, in spite of their distressingly fatuous speeches, in spite of their foolish faces absurdly distorted by the need to keep up appearances, the bond that unites us is as big as the universe, oh my life-tarnished beloveds, how I'd love to kiss you, to hypnotise you with delight, to overwhelm you with kindness, even you, my darling Rorty, noxious little whore to the great god capital, vile little taxman's toad, I am floating above your speech, riding your enthusiasm, the plan to build a roof terrace on the tenth floor has made great progress, it is going to include a swimming pool, a café and a little garden looking out over the whole of Paris, the work is almost finished, we will soon be inviting the press, the directors of all our subsidiaries around the world will be able to meet there, it's fantastic, it's wonderful, the poignant beauty of Tissier, Stoeffer, Pujol, Brémont, Castaglione, Meyer, de Vals,

Clément-Dourville and Roussel as they hear this news, the plan to build a roof terrace on the tenth floor has made great progress, there will be a swimming pool, a café and a little garden looking out over the whole of Paris, the work is almost finished, we will soon be inviting the press, the directors of all our subsidiaries around the world will be able to meet there, and as for us, the magic of simply saying so will allow us to meet up there in a fraction of a second, all eleven of us, up there, towering over Paris, O language, immeasurable power of the word, O my Rorty, so handsome, so proud of your roof terrace, my little sun-god looking out over the whole of Paris, O sweet Rorty, if you knew how little I give a damn about your roof-terrace-building plans but how much I love you, you, mullah of open spaces, emperor of corporate communications, I love you as much as the shimmering angels made of sky and light that I see within you, within you all, I am happy, just so happy to be here, I am happy, just so happy to be alive, the walls are shining, the air becoming more intense, argon, oxygen, nitrogen, you are my friends, atoms of love are beaming through the whole building, everything sends me into raptures, every sight enchants me and I'm no longer frightened of anything, not of picking up the phone to call prospective customers and hearing that they've chosen another company, not of being summoned by Rorty to learn that, as I'm the least productive member of staff, a decision – which in no way reflects on my professional competency – will have to be taken about me, who cares if I leave this company, after all, life is good, what does it matter, haven't I always planned to take a sabbatical at some stage, take stock, reread Eckhart, Wittgenstein, St Augustine, Musil, Dostoevsky, Kafka, or else radically change career, it doesn't matter, it all seems equal and wonderful to me, every possibility enchanting, the sky is beautiful, with great majestic clouds drifting gently across it, such beauty, I could spend my whole life looking at them, the mineral, animal and vegetable united once more, an invisible party celebrating every pulsation of life, infinity is right here, eternity is within reach, it all seems equal and wonderful to me, even the thought of having to die one day, relax my dear ones, I am here to bring you the good news, we are all alive, that is the good news, tonight I'm seeing Agnès and Marc, perhaps we'll go to the movies and then out to dinner, and then each back to our own place, and sleep, and wake up to go to work, heads full of dreams and possibilities, all this is totally banal yet fills me with unexpected delight, the most ordinary daily life is a miracle, the miracle of knowing one is alive, as stupid as that, last night I thought I was going to die and yet I'm here, alive, I can still see the car with extraordinary clarity, in slow motion, a black BMW with tinted windows, I can feel the vibration of the sub-woofer, feel the heavy, metallic techno-rap creeping into my veins like an adrenalin-flavoured poison, two men stepped out, one large and muscular, the other short and lean, strangely the little one reminded me of my mother, I saw a pistol in his pocket, heard the words dirty poof, you're dead meat, when I saw him train his gun on me my heart started racing and my blood froze, I thought of all the people killed for ridiculous reasons, the refusal of a cigarette, a bolshy glance or simply because the killers didn't like the look of them, all those people killed for nothing, in the street or an underground station, I heard sniggers in the car, the man went to squeeze the trigger, his features were tense, he was wearing sunglasses and a leather jacket, the more he aimed the more tense he became and the more fear rose up in me, a primitive, almost animal fear, a feeling from the beginning of time, common to all species, an unfamiliar feeling which suddenly transformed into a strange kind of ecstatic peace, as if the scene concerned somebody else, as if the little me of my usual life had been replaced by another me capable of gliding above my physical body, surveying space, time and all of experience in the blink of an eye, then the fleeting sight of a street lamp followed by a metallic dizziness, the sensation of falling, then loss of consciousness and return to life lying on the tarmac, the street lamp again, and simultaneously cars, headlights, fast-food joints, trees, cafés, a distant police siren, it was dawn, a passer-by stopped to help me, he reminded me of Carlos, I thought of asking him if he enjoyed walking around the area with his showbiz friends but I contented myself with replying that everything was fine, thanks, I stood up and set off for my apartment, dishevelled but alive, I started walking, slowly at first, then at a good pace, the further I walked the more I saw the world in slow motion and my own life speeded up, the sheltered, intimate years of primary school, the tar-flavoured pain of falling off my bike, the explosive delight of exam results, the splendour and mystery of books both sacred and profane, climbing through the mist to the Tibetan summits in the footsteps of Alexandra David-Neel, and outside the city was filing past in pleasant little scenes, the young woman with the umbrella walking her dog, the dustman running behind the green truck, the taxi driver beeping his horn and swearing at everything, after another few miles, home, how long did I sleep, an hour, maybe two, in any case long enough to have that waking dream, like something out of a fantastical, initiatory novel by Hesse, Lovecraft, Castaneda or Philip K. Dick, after it happened a few titles jostled through my mind, *If You Find This World Bad You Should See the Others, Ubik, Do Androids Dream of Electric Sheep, The Teachings of Don Juan, Journey to Ixtlan, Tales of Power, The Power of Silence, Steppenwolf*, I say after it happened but in fact what happened, nothing, or so little, really almost nothing, to start with just a feeling, the strange sensation of not being alone, in my bedroom, a sensation that immediately became a certainty, I wasn't alone, a secret meeting was taking place, about a foot above my head, as if a meeting room had suddenly taken up residence there, slipped in, a meeting room full of invisible but noisy participants, what an absurd idea I exclaimed mid-dream, but at the same time I could hear them chirruping, screeching, sighing, one of them even congratulated himself mysteriously on the pioneering gynaeco-cosmologies, heralds of a better future, what pioneering gynaeco-cosmologies I asked myself, rational as anything, and anyway, who were these beings, so well informed about divine intention, fairies, goblins, djinns and the like, where in the world could I find them, how could I get back on the right path, is there a right path, I suddenly thought of Rudolf Steiner and his theory of subtle worlds, confused dimensions inhabited by invisible, age-old, conscious entities, the meeting room disappeared to make way for a maze of corridors and darkened rooms, in one of the rooms, on a chest of drawers, in an art nouveau frame, was Magda's face, with short urchin hair, smiling at me, the frame started to speak with my own voice, Magda's hairstyle suddenly changed, from an urchin she became a resistance fighter, then a 1950s femme fatale, then a hippie with a purple headband, a tangled mass of hair and round John Lennon glasses, and though it was mine, the voice had the mechanical, inhuman dullness of voicemail, banking services, recorded messages and computer games, she was telling me that it wasn't such a big deal that we'd separated, after all I was neither the first nor the last, I replied that she was right, life is not a tragedy, things always turn out OK, then I bumped into something, instead of corridors and darkened rooms there was a tree, a solitary oak in a sunlit field, it was alive, quivering, radiant, and then I found myself back on the living-room sofa, strangely serene, detached and full of love for the sofa, the room, the city, the world, the galaxy, our day-to-day worries and mean-minded concerns are so unimportant compared to the power that is everywhere and in everyone, these payment due dates and formal notices are so stupidly trivial compared to the radiant flood carrying not only me, but also Rorty, de Vals, Castaglione, Meyer, Roussel and the others, it's all so fragile and yet so simple, heavens their gloomy faces are amusing, those starchy expressions are screaming out for a spanking, or for someone to burst out laughing, I'd so love to kiss them, cuddle them, take a gun, aim it at their head and then shoot just to one side, to make them realise that nothing is serious, we are just passing through, so fluid, so light, just yesterday I was always complaining, worrying, my break-up, my prospects, my place in next year's organisational hierarchy, rumours, gossip, am I no longer in favour, will losing the AGH account have affected Rorty's trust in me, he is building up to a big round of redundancies, will I be one of them, all that seems so distant, so laughable compared to the immeasurable power of the moment, I had to come face to face with death in order to love life, hey, that reminds me of a film, yes, that's right, Capra's *It's a Wonderful Life,* about that banker up to his ears in debt and despair who asks an angel to make him invisible, the angel grants him his wish but the man can't stop haunting the places he knew and the people he loved, he can see them, he tries desperately to speak to them but no one hears him, suddenly the problems that had once overwhelmed him seem infinitely preferable to this endless solitude, yes, that's right,

I remember, the man asks the angel to bring him back to life and all's well that ends well, a parable about grace and the will to live, even in the midst of death and chaos, even if existence is an enchanted island in the middle of a wild and raging sea, nothing and nobody will be able to take away the fact that THAT happened one day, on this earth, this welcoming, generous earth on which we are nothing but guests, don't let's forget, let's never forget, this earth wreathed in glory and swarming with mystery, O my adorable corporate goblins, smash through the dry dullness of confined spaces to find the joy lurking inside you, the spirit that is knocking every second but that you never hear, deafened as you are by the roar of stress, oh Tissier, I see you, grouchy Tissier, sweet Tissier, hey Rorty baby, peek-a-boo Castaglione sweetie pie, I love you all infinitely, oh, they're so cute, looking down at me from the heights of their haughty ignorance of the world's beauty, open your eyes my friends, open your eyes to the miracle of the night, the inevitable has been reversed and death transformed into life, who were those guys, where had they come from, did they really intend to kill me or was it all bluff, a theatrical scene among friends, and in the first hypothesis do I owe my life to police presence or, more likely I'm sure, to a simple technical problem, an empty magazine or misfiring pistol, but then it doesn't matter, the main thing is that I'm alive, conscious and full of joy, with Rorty still crowing about his plan to build a roof terrace that looks out over the whole of Paris, it will be the perfect place to meet clients, and that silly goose Castaglione flattering him, gushing her approval, it's the company's most important project, so wonderful for hosting clients, prospects, journalists, artists, company directors, politicians, and just perfect for breakfast briefings, Rorty nods, with a hint of a smile, I feel as if I'm smiling too, I'm sure of it, I'm smiling, smiling at Rorty, Rorty, surprised, smiles back at me, unless he's just continuing to smile for some reason unrelated to my own smile, who cares, I smile at Rorty who smiles at me, Rorty is glancing back at me, he looks surprised, almost shocked, Castaglione is looking at me, she seems surprised too, she's watching me closely, watching Rorty's reaction, the woman is a vestal virgin, Rorty is her god, a god she will soon destroy and sacrifice to the glory of Thanatos, poor dear Rorty, you are the Venus in her flytrap, the moth fluttering around her deadly light, the innocent lamb bleating before her hungry wolf, your destiny awaits you, you are rushing towards it, whistling, sure of your power and unaware of the danger she poses to you, poor, poor dear Rorty, my handsome fawn with your baby's bottom, if only you knew what any animal documentary could tell you, the biggest predators always end up being devoured, I can see the two of you making love in a blood-coloured bedroom, power games, rifts, confrontations, there will only be one winner and it won't be you, I'm sure of that, no question, I can read the future as easily as the present, the past or the air around me, in a week, maybe two, Castaglione will invite you over to her place, a smart apartment in the sixteenth with a view of the Eiffel Tower, weak with desire you will accept, and very soon succumb to her mystery, you will be gobbled up, the alpha male will become once more as tiny as the spermatozoid he once was, return to the human soup, to the beauty of the primordial, I am still smiling, Rorty smiles no more . . .

1pm: the chairman
declares the meeting closed.

penguin.co.uk/vintage